Baruch Elias

Baruch Elias is a lucky man. At twenty-three he has pretty much everything he wants including the girl he hopes to marry. But life never runs so smooth. When a rider races into the yard with some devastating news, he has to unravel a fire, a family secret, a fatal accident and work out how all that fits together. A pair of ridge riders and a fatal shooting put Baruch in grave danger, while a corrupt lawman complicates everything. Fast on the draw and a crack shot, but headstrong and inexperienced, Baruch lets his heart rule his head and that can only lead to one thing . . . more trouble.

Baruch Elias

Frank Chandler

A Black Horse Western

ROBERT HALE

© Frank Chandler 2019
First published in Great Britain 2019

ISBN 978-0-7198-3005-1

The Crowood Press
The Stable Block
Crowood Lane
Ramsbury
Marlborough
Wiltshire SN8 2HR

www.bhwesterns.com

Robert Hale is an imprint
of The Crowood Press

1

Baruch Elias knew he was a lucky man. The sun was up and the air was warm. A gentle breeze carried the intermittent call of a cactus wren across the valley. A good herd of beef was stirring by the watercourse. Tall stands of corn flourished in soil watered by a snow-fed river, little more than a stream through the summer. Southwest Utah does not have the best of farming country. It is for the most part dry, rugged, deeply gouged by canyons and generally unkind to both settlers and travellers. But it is not all badlands and hoodoos; there are parts where a living can be carved out of the colourful ground. Here and there, brakes of willow and cottonwood follow the sparse tracts of water. Ponderosa pine, bigtooth maples, aspens and ancient bristlecones grow side by side on the precipitous slopes, the lower parts being covered with yucca, cactus and a mix of brushwood, junipers, needle grass and sagebrush. In places, the open ground provides just about enough grazing for cattle.

In its own way, the land stretching out in front of Baruch looked good. But the ranch wasn't his, nor the crops or the beeves. They all belonged to the father of the pretty young woman who was riding out with him early on that fine summer morning. That was why he knew himself to be lucky.

Ingrid pulled her horse up and brought them both to a halt. 'Don't say you got me up early just to see our own cows taking a morning drink.'

'Of course not,' Baruch replied with a laugh. 'I just wanted to do a bit of shooting, and for us to see the sunrise together.'

'Well, we're too late for that.'

Ingrid dropped the reins over the horse's head, slid down from the saddle and turned it loose to munch the grass. 'Anyway, I don't believe a word of it. There's something on your mind. You've been like a rattlesnake with a sore tail for the last week. What's eating you?'

Baruch got off his horse and took hold of Ingrid straight away, firmly and affectionately. He leant down to kiss her, but she turned her head.

'Not until you tell me what's on your mind.'

'Listen, Ingrid, I'm twenty-three and you're nineteen and your pa knows we want to get married. The time is right and I'm sure your pa will give his blessing.'

'You know he will.'

Baruch let go of Ingrid and turned his back on her. 'But there is something I have to tell you. Something your pa has to know and it might make him change his mind.'

'Never! You're like a son to him. You've been with us for quite a while now, and worked for almost nothing, just food and a bed.' She looked wistful. 'Or was it all a scheme just to get me for your wife?'

Baruch smiled at her. Ingrid was a beauty in her own way. She had a wonderful character that could see the funny side of everything and always saw the good in everyone. Perhaps that naïve innocence was what attracted Baruch more than her long blonde hair, blue eyes, fresh complexion and the steely Swedish core that she inherited from her father. Put together, these attributes made her an irresistible catch.

'Ingrid, when I came to your pa, four years ago, to get me away from . . . from something I'm ashamed to talk about, you were nothing more than an awkward gangling, clumsy tomboy with a toothy smile that made me laugh.'

'And look at me now!' Ingrid said with a shrug of self-indulgent pleasure.

But Baruch was being serious. He took his rifle out of he saddle holster and fed it with bullets from his belt. 'Would your pa still sanction our marriage if I said I didn't want to stay on the ranch? If I said I thought there was a better life for us somewhere else?'

'Somewhere else? You know I couldn't leave my dad. I'm all the family he's got since my mother passed away. You wouldn't ask me to leave him, would you?'

7

'You see that post sticking up over there?'

'No.'

'Way over between those two yucca.'

'Yes, I see it.'

Baruch levelled the gun sight and squeezed the trigger. A puff of smoke left the end of the barrel along with a piece of hot lead going too fast to see. But the post felt it when it smacked into the wood, sending a shower of splinters into the air.

'Bravo!' Ingrid said clapping her hands and smiling.

'Raising beef and crops and whatever isn't all that much fun for a man like me.'

'Like you? What d'you mean, Baruch? A man like you? A gunfighter?'

'Hell, no, I don't want to be no gunfighter, but I want a better life for you and me and our children. You do want children, don't you, Ingrid?'

'Yes,' she said, hesitating, 'lots, but I want them to grow up on this ranch, like I have. I want them always to have good food on the table, to learn their letters and look after our animals. Grow up to be good people, respect the land that provides for them. It's a good life, Baruch.'

'Yes, a good life, but is it enough?'

'Do you mean, am I enough?'

'No, I don't mean that at all.'

Ingrid was missing the point. Baruch reloaded the Winchester with a sharp downward pull on the mechanism and fired three more shots in quick succession. Splinters flew everywhere, and on the third shot the top of the post fell away completely.

The sharp shooting wasn't lost on Ingrid, but she was concerned. 'Are you angry? Shooting like that?'

'No, I'm not angry, just restless. You see, I have to tell your pa about Ferdy.'

'Who's Ferdy?'

'He was my baby brother.'

'Was?'

'Yes, that's what I have to tell your pa about. I can't have any secrets from him if I'm asking him for his daughter to be my wife. He'll want to be sure I'm going to treat you right. He has to know everything.'

Ingrid frowned. 'You'd treat me right, wouldn't you?'

'Of course.'

Baruch's bottom lip began to tremble. There was nothing he was afraid of, nothing he wouldn't stand up to, but whenever he thought of Ferdy's dreadful accident he could scarcely hold back his emotion.

'You all right, Baruch?'

'I'm fine,' he replied, more brusquely than he meant.

He looked down sorrowfully and his mind's eye suddenly saw the crumpled figure, the smashed skull, the pool of blood.

He put the rifle back in the holster, stepped forward, away from Ingrid and stood still, legs spread, his arms at his side, right arm slightly lower. Then suddenly his right hand flashed upwards, whipped out his six-gun on the rise, and blasted off four shots at what was left of the post.

9

It was almost out of range for the nicely balanced Remington .36 with its polished wood grip, but two of the four shots hit the stump with a satisfying thud. Ingrid thought it was a poor show to miss with two bullets, but she had no idea that to hit the post at that range was a feat of considerable marksmanship.

She turned to Baruch. 'Why do you keep practising with your guns? We don't get many predators round here.'

'No, just occasional coyotes and sometimes a wolf, but you never know. One day I might be glad of the practice.'

Ingrid shook her head. 'You know what I think Baruch, I think you want to be a bank robber.' She laughed out loud.

Baruch was indignant. 'I do not. No such thing, Ingrid. I just want to be sure I can protect you if the need ever arises.'

He took her in his arms to kiss, and this time she didn't turn away but melted into his chest. In that moment Baruch knew he would never let anyone or anything come between them.

'Promise you won't shoot your guns at anyone in anger.'

'Of course not. Why would I ever want to do that?'

'Well, you keep practising. It's got to be for something.'

Baruch hoped he'd never need to use his gun in that way. It was just in case, if ever . . . if ever.

'I have to tell your pa about Ferdy. He must say if he thinks I'm good enough for you. I can't let this go

BARUCH ELIAS

on unless I know he will accept me for his son-in-law, to be the husband of his daughter. We both know how he dotes on you. You are all the family he has, you are the living memory of his wife, the mother you hardly knew.'

'That was a long time ago,' Ingrid assured him. 'You know she died on the journey to America. I was only two or three. You must have been about six. When I got older, I hoped Pa would find another wife. I used to pray to God for it every night. Maybe in town or somewhere, there would be someone to make his life whole again. Vimy Point is only a short ride from here but he hardly ever goes there except for supplies. Angelina comes round to do some housework and cook fine meals. I know he likes to see her, but she is like one of the family and he doesn't go out of his way to meet people. I know he misses my mother dreadfully. Sometimes, I think people may only love once in their life and nobody else can fill that void when they are gone. Is that how you would love me?'

'I would love you to the ends of the earth, you know that.'

'Then that's all that matters. Pa won't think any the worse of you whatever it is that you want to tell him about Ferdy. Are you sure he doesn't know already?'

Baruch wanted to say more – there was so much more to say, so much guilt to shed – but he didn't want to bring all his sadness into the moment. It happened on Ferdy's birthday of all days; he was no

11

more than an eager lad when he died. It broke Baruch's heart to feel he was responsible for the accident.

He gave Ingrid a brief hug to clear the memory. They mounted up and rode back to the ranch.

Breakfast was a tense situation. The only noise was from Angelina at the stove. When the meal was finished, they were sitting uncomfortably, wondering who was going to say something. Baruch took a piece of corn bread and mopped up the last of the gravy from his plate. Ingrid put her fork down quietly. She sat silently with her hands in her lap, but her eyes were trying to catch Baruch's attention. She knew he wanted to start the conversation with her father but she couldn't start it herself, nor find a way to get it started for him.

For his part, Ingrid's father, Arnie Sigurrson, knew something was in the air. The conversation during the meal had not flowed as freely as usual; it had been hesitant, almost formal. He knew Baruch had something important to say. He took out a small knife to cut the end off a fine cigar but in his anxiety made a mess of it and cursed. He slammed the knife on the table and angrily threw the cigar in the fire.

Red-faced, he turned to Baruch. 'Well, spit it out, young man, what is it you want to say? Something's going on, I know it.'

'Yes, sir, I've been wanting to tell you quite a while, but haven't found the right moment.'

Suddenly there was a commotion outside, and a

rider raced into the yard. There was a violent knock on the door.

Arnie got up at once, taking the shotgun off the hook, and went to the door. He shouted the warning that he was carrying a loaded shotgun, then lifted the latch. The rider looked exhausted: beads of sweat were gathered on his brow. He pulled his neckerchief from under his collar and began to dab at the drops.

'Is Baruch here?' the man spluttered.

'Who wants him?' Arnie replied.

'I'm Jake Gilling, neighbour to his folks in Vendigo Bluff. I've urgent news. I've ridden hard through day and night. It's about his parents, Nils and Hedda Elias.'

Baruch leapt up from the table and went to the door.

'Jake! What's the news?'

'Your parents, Baruch. Their hardware store has been smashed up. Your pa's in a bad way.'

Arnie invited Jake into the house and sat him down at the table. Ingrid fetched a mug of water and then stood beside Baruch. They waited for Jake to drain the water and recover his breath. He dabbed at the sweat.

'I'm right sorry to bring you this news, Baruch. But your ma told me where you were and asked me to get to you as soon as I could.'

'Is she all right?'

'She is, yes, kinda. But your pa's taken a bad beating. And the store's all smashed up, burnt out

. . . everything's lost. The biggest shebang in Vendigo, now just a shell.'

'But is Pa going to be all right?'

Jake didn't answer, just pursed his lips and looked away.

Baruch wasted no time making a decision. He turned to Arnie. 'I have to go to them.'

Arnie nodded. 'I understand, lad. I'm right sorry to hear this, and of course you want to go back and help them.' He put his hand on his daughter's shoulder while keeping eye contact with Baruch. 'Harvest is coming up and the cattle drive will have to start soon. You take as long as you need. I guess we'll just have to manage for a while. What can we do to help?'

Baruch turned to Jake. 'Do they know who did this?'

'Oh, yes, they know all right. No question about it. It was Erik, bold as brass, and a few other no-goods to back him up.'

'Uncle Erik! Pa's brother. . . . Why? I thought he was still in jail.'

'I don't know. You'll have to ask your folks about that. All I know is that the sheriff knew it was Erik. He rode into town, went into the store and came out later all fired up shooting off his gun, left right and centre. Then he rampaged up Main Street hollering and whooping, and shouting out what he was going to do. Then he went right on and did it. Smashed the place up then set it alight.'

Baruch was silent, trying not to imagine the scene

that kept coming to him like a nightmare.

Jake continued. 'And you know what? The sheriff was standing there in the street and didn't lift a finger to do nuthin' about it. Just watched the store burn. Folk were running round with buckets of water and doing what they could, but there was no saving the store or the goods inside.'

All eyes were downcast. Arnie Sigurrson broke the silence.

'It's a terrible loss for you, Baruch. It'll feel like a punishment for leaving your folks alone. When Mira died in childbirth it felt like I was being punished for leaving my homeland to come to this country. The Almighty took away my wife, the son she was going to have, and my dreams with it. It was a boy, you know. The doc couldn't save either of them. I was suddenly left alone with only little Ingrid to care for.'

'I was a comfort to you, Pa,' Ingrid said somewhat defensively, giving him a kiss on the cheek.

'Yes, I know. I know. And you've looked after me very well all these years, and grown into a fine young woman.'

Baruch cleared his throat. 'And that's something else, sir.'

Arnie knew what was coming next. He was pleased and not pleased, he had tried to delay the inevitable announcement. 'You will come back, won't you Baruch? You're like my own son, you know. And everything will carry on just as before. . . .'

'I'd like to marry Ingrid, sir.'

It was blurted out in a way that was never intended. He'd rehearsed it over and over in his head, all polite and calm and as mature as he could be at twenty-three. But when it came to it he'd thrown it out like a challenge, and with a guest in the house as well.

'I'm sorry, Mr Sigursson, I never meant it to sound like that.'

'Of course you didn't, boy. Nobody ever does, but however it comes, it'll always be a shock to a father. All you ever wish for a daughter is that she marries a good man who'll look after her and love her and raise a family and always be kind to her.'

'I can promise all that, sir.'

'I know. And I couldn't wish for a better man for Ingrid. If she'll have you!'

'Of course I will, Pa, and it means he'll come back soon!'

Despite this rushed conversation and seemingly happy outcome, Baruch was eager to get going. 'I must pack and get off. Rest assured, Mr Sigursson, I will be back as soon as I can.'

Baruch offered his hand but Arnie pulled him into an embrace.

'You are part of the family in every respect, Baruch. I wish you well, take care, stay safe and we will be waiting your return.'

Baruch took his leave to pack, and tears formed in Ingrid's eyes. Wistfully, Arnie opened the box on the table and took out a cigar. He took up the knife again and calmly cut the end. Angelina got up and cleared the plates. Arnie put a light to his cigar, and then blew out a thick stream of blue-grey smoke.

'I guess you'd like some breakfast,' he said to Jake.

2

Baruch didn't know what to make of the news; so many things were swirling round in his head. He tried to dismiss the images that kept flashing into his mind: his pa being beaten, his ma being helpless to do anything, the store being ransacked and razed. But worst of all was the thought that this wasn't some mindless act of a group of no-good ridge riders fired up with booze and bravado – this was something altogether unbelievably puzzling, because it was his pa's own brother, Erik, who had committed this dreadful act. But why?

Baruch cut a sorry figure tying up his bedroll and putting together his coffee pot, tin mug, strikers and small pack of supplies. He carried them out to the stable and saddled his horse, a fine black quarter horse jokingly named Whitey because of two white feet. He chucked the reins over Whitey's neck so he could slip the bridle over the ears and secured the curb bit over the horse's tongue. Ready to go, he checked the rifle and topped up the bullets. He took

18

two boxes of shells from the store, .44 for the rifle and .36 for his handgun. One day he'd buy a new handgun that took the same as the Winchester. He danced his fingers over the shelves and took three packs of tobacco. He'd not been to see his parents since he left four years ago, since that dreadful day when he realized he was the cause of Ferdy's accident. He'd always wanted to go back home and see his parents, but he couldn't bring himself to face them. He'd always known how they felt about his little brother Ferdy. He always believed Ferdy was their favourite.

He was wallowing in self-pity when Ingrid came out to the stable.

'Baruch, you will be back won't you? And you will take care of yourself. You could wait for Jake and he'd ride with you.'

'His horse won't be ready for a couple of days after his hard ride. It's going to take me about three days to get to Vendigo Bluff and the sooner I leave the better. Besides, I couldn't sit around here knowing they needed my help. I'll find that sonofabitch and, uncle or not, I'll bring him to justice.'

'But you will be careful,' Ingrid pleaded.

Baruch took her in his arms and they kissed warmly, not knowing when they might see each other again.

'Have you ever doubted me?'

Revenge is a powerful thing and can lead to rash decisions and hasty action. Ingrid shook her head; there were tears in her eyes. She couldn't speak for

19

choking on the fear of Baruch blindly chasing justice, being overconfident, and getting himself killed.

He swung up into the saddle and trotted out of the yard. Ingrid was clutching her dress like a small child filled with anxiety. Baruch looked back at her briefly and waved his hat before urging his horse into a canter.

Ingrid burst into tears.

That first day was a long hot ride. The sun beat down mercilessly, with long periods of walking and trotting interspersed with cantering where the road was good and flat. By the time he decided to stop for the night, Baruch had made good progress.

Radford was little more than a two-bit town where a little wooden bridge crossed a dried riverbed. But it had a building that rather grandly called itself a hotel. A few stores, a ramshackle saloon, barbershop and livery stable with feed merchant was about all it had to offer. But that was all Baruch needed. He settled his horse in livery and walked over to the hotel. He checked in and then crossed the road to the saloon.

The room went quiet as he pushed in through the batwings. All eyes turned towards him. The barkeep watched to see how Baruch would react. It didn't look like a particularly welcoming sight. Unwilling to be deterred by the apparent hostility to strangers, standing tall, he walked over to the counter.

'Glass of beer, please.'

The room relaxed. They were impressed with this young man's demeanour. The town was used to travellers, strangers, honest folk and outlaws alike. They treated them all with a cold scrutiny until they had the measure of the visitor's intent. If they were satisfied, the room would carry on. If not, someone would stand up and challenge with a few well-chosen words.

In this case they could see Baruch was not the type to be an outlaw. He looked honest enough in his plainsman's hat and was not carrying a side arm, so was accorded a welcome by being left alone. It didn't feel much like a welcome to Baruch until the barkeep spoke.

'You're welcome, son. Just passing through?'

Baruch nodded. 'On my way to Vendigo Bluff.'

'That's a long ride. You got business there?'

'My folks have a hardware store. Some tearaways have burnt them out.'

'Sorry to hear that. What's your name?'

'Elias, Baruch Elias.'

'Well, how d'yer do? I'm Bryce Radford, owner of this establishment.'

'Same name as the town,' Baruch observed.

'Yep. My grandfather settled here after fighting Indians and set up a trading post. I'm third generation. Guess you've checked into my hotel across the road, and you've put your horse in my livery.' He laughed. 'Yes, I own most of this place thanks to my folks. Now I guess you'll want to eat. My wife's got a good stew going. Take a seat and I'll bring some over.'

That was much more of a warm welcome, and better than many people got, although Baruch wouldn't have known it. He couldn't blame them for being cautious: the stagecoach didn't often stop in Radford, and the roads were frequented by traders and hucksters, highway robbers and outlaws on the dodge. It never did to be anything less than wary of strangers.

The stew was almost as good as those that Angelina made back on the Sigurrson ranch. The thought of Ingrid and her pa tucking into their evening meal, with Jake as a guest, made him very homesick after just one day away. Strange, because the ranch wasn't his home – he'd only been there four years – and what did he have of a family home in Vendigo? Just a burnt-out shell. He'd never felt so alone as he did that night sliding under the covers in the hotel bedroom.

The next day started with a good breakfast in the saloon across the road. Two-bit town it may be, but Bryce's wife produced damn good grub. Although the hotel bed wasn't as comfortable as the one he was used to at the ranch, the overnight was better than he'd feared. At least, that was the case until his breakfast was rudely interrupted by a couple of roughnecks who pushed into the saloon and started mouthing off at Bryce, not realising he was the owner of the saloon and most of the town.

'What a lousy hole this town is. Don't s'pose you got any grub for two hungry travellers. God, what a dump!'

Bryce Radford swallowed his pride and answered them politely. 'As a matter of fact, we do. So if you two gentlemen would like to sit yourselves down, I'll bring you something to eat.'

They turned round to look for somewhere to sit and clapped eyes on Baruch.

'What yer eatin', boy?'

Baruch would have preferred to ignore them but couldn't sidestep a direct question. 'Pancakes and syrup.'

'That's what I used to give to my hogs, make them big and fat, but you're a skinny little runt. How's that?'

'Guess I'm not a hog,' Baruch replied, wishing he hadn't been so smart.

'Well, son, you look like one to me.'

This was possibly the end of a peaceful breakfast. Baruch was not wearing his holster and six-gun because, as a stranger in town, he didn't wish to look like a gunslinger or outlaw. He very much regretted that decision. It was a lesson learned too late. He should never be without a means of defence, however peaceful the place might seem. Something like this could happen anywhere at any time. It was obvious to Baruch that these two were just out looking for trouble. Probably a couple of wanted ridge riders, they'd had a bad night's sleep and were itching to take it out on somebody.

Baruch looked like easy prey. His mind was whirling round all the ways of getting out of the situation. Nothing looked promising.

The man spoke roughly again. 'I said you remind me of my hogs,' he repeated walking across to Baruch's table.

'You must have mighty fine hogs!'

The man turned to his friend and smiled. 'Don't he remind you of my hogs, Abel? That big pink snout, those little beady eyes and the squealin'?'

Suddenly Bryce took the shotgun from under the counter and levelled it at the backs of the two men.

'That's enough! Keep your hands away from your guns and just walk out nice and slow. Mount up and git out of our town. You ain't no better than swine yourself, so clear out.'

Sensibly, the two men held their hands away from their sides and walked to the batwings. Abel, the silent one, was just about to go out when, stupidly, his mouthy companion pulled his gun and, swinging round, blasted a shot towards Bryce. The shotgun retaliated immediately and the mouthy fool was thrown clean out, crashing through the batwings and into the street.

Before the other man could draw his gun, Baruch was out of his chair and aimed one huge swing, connecting perfectly under his jaw. The man's neck seemed to stretch an extra couple of inches as his head went back and his eyes closed. He fell to the ground in an untidy heap.

'Blasted vermin!' Bryce complained. 'Look at the mess on the wall. Trouble is this town's not big enough for a sheriff and we have to do all the damn dirty work ourselves.'

Baruch accompanied Bryce into the street to see what was left of the other man. It wasn't a pretty sight. He was dead, no two ways about it. The blood-stained hole was witness to that. Bryce fished about in the man's slicker and found a piece of folded paper in one of the pockets.

'Well, look at that,' he said, passing the paper to Baruch. 'He's carrying a reward dodger, but he ain't no bounty hunter. D'you reckon the drawing is of him?'

Baruch took the poster. It offered a reward for the Benson brothers, Kane and Abel: a thousand dollars each. 'I guess they're the Bensons.'

Bryce was already on his way back into the saloon. The other man, who'd been called Abel, was just coming round and moaning like crazy. His hand was gingerly exploring his jaw, which was evidently extremely painful.

'You lousy . . .' was as much as he managed to say before Bryce prodded him in the chest with the shotgun.

'Your name Benson?' Bryce demanded. 'Abel Benson?'

'What's it to you?'

Baruch held out the dodger. 'A thousand dollars, according to this.'

The man spat, despite the obvious pain that the action caused to his jaw.

Bryce called out to his wife. 'Mary-Lou! Bring me some restraining rope.'

He turned to Baruch. 'Get this outlaw tied up and

we might just be doing our good deed for the day.'

The shotgun ensured the compliance of the man who was assumed to be one of the two Benson brothers on the dodger. Although he struggled a lot, not wanting to give in too easily, Baruch soon had him hogtied securely.

'Learned that on the ranch,' he said to the man. 'Useful when you work with hogs.'

The irony was lost on the outlaw, who spat again onto the floor as a mark of his disgust with the outcome of the morning. No doubt he was rueing his brother's bad manners that cost him his life and lost Abel his chance of a breakfast. On closer scrutiny of the rough sketch on the dodger, there was not much doubt these were the Benson brothers. Kane looked a bit like the dead one and Abel was tied up good. The only question now was how to get them both to a sheriff and claim the reward.

Bryce Radford replaced the one spent cartridge in the shotgun and put it back under the counter.

'We'd better get that corpse off the street before it brings in all the flies from miles around.'

Bryce led Baruch outside and they quickly dispersed the small crowd of onlookers who were trying to identify the fallen man.

'He ain't one of us,' someone said.

'Ridge rider on the dodge,' said another. 'Long hair, old stubble, bad teeth, seen 'em all, an' they all look like that.'

'Step back, folks,' Bryce said, taking control. It seemed to Baruch that in the absence of a sheriff,

Bryce Radford was probably the nearest thing to a lawman that the town possessed. He was clearly the most eminent citizen.

They dragged the man off the street, round the back of the saloon and wrapped him in a piece of old tarp.

'Now then,' Bryce began, 'I guess those two horses hitched across the street belong to these men. We'd best take a look at what's in the saddle-bags. Bring 'em over to the saloon.'

Baruch slipped the saddle-bags off both horses and chucked them down on the bar counter. Bryce opened one and Baruch opened the other.

Bryce let out a whoop, 'Geez!' He pulled out bundles of dollar bills tied up into packages. 'This is some stash!'

Although Baruch heard what Bryce said, he was far more interested in a box that he'd taken out of the other saddle-bags. Inside there were bits and pieces of insignia and half a dozen tunic buttons from a military jacket. There was a piece of material with a sergeant's stripes and, underneath that, a dented powder case. At the bottom of the box was a small quantity of jewellery, a couple of dress rings, a necklace, three brooches and one or two more small rings with stones. But it was the simple gold wedding ring that Baruch was looking at. It was a broad ring made for a man. The inside was engraved with two names, Nils and Hedda, with a date, June 7th, 1847.

'What you got there?' Bryce asked having got to the bottom of the bag he was searching. 'There must be several thousand dollars here. Looks like they've been involved in a recent robbery. You'll have to ask the sheriff when you get to Vendigo. Meanwhile, I'll look after this loot.'

Baruch heard what Bryce said, but he wasn't listening. He turned the ring round in his hand and kept looking at it.

'I know this ring,' he said wistfully. 'I know exactly where this has come from.'

'You do?'

But Baruch only said, 'I'll hold onto this.' He slipped the ring into his pocket.

'You can take this man and his dead brother with you to Vendigo Bluff. It's the nearest place with a lawman that could pay out the reward. You're on your way there, aren't you? They can lock them up there. When you come back this way, you can give me my share. Now let's get back inside. You need some fresh breakfast and coffee.'

Baruch promised to bring Bryce's reward money on his return journey, but before he sat down he took his gunbelt out of his saddle-bag and strapped it on. He checked the cylinder on the gun and slid it into the holster. Lightning doesn't strike twice, but if it did, he was going to be ready for whatever happened next.

After Mary-Lou had provided a very satisfying hot second breakfast and two mugs of good steaming coffee, Baruch paid for the lodging and food, saddled up his own horse and took the two confiscated horses. He loaded up the wrapped corpse on one and sat Abel, no longer hogtied, on the other, securing his hands to the saddle horn. He walked them out into the street. It was a fine warm morning, with a light breeze blowing from the west.

Bryce and Mary-Lou were standing outside the saloon. He was in his bright white apron with his arms folded across his chest, a decent proud man, salt of the earth, honest and fearless. Mary-Lou had linked their arms affectionately. Baruch waved a salute as he passed by, which Bryce acknowledged by nodding his head. Mary-Lou smiled and waved. They watched Baruch head out of town with two extra horses, one corpse and one prisoner.

Bryce squeezed his wife, and then he sighed and frowned. 'He's got a tough journey ahead of him to get that cargo safely to the sheriff at Vendigo Bluff.'

For Baruch, too, the thousand-dollar reward was not what was uppermost in his mind, nor the fact that Bryce trusted him to bring back his share of the reward: both those things made Baruch feel good. But what was on his mind was that the journey to Vendigo Bluff was probably two days' ride, and although his prisoner was tied up he presented a real danger. Not only was he alive and ready to see every opportunity for escape, but worse than that there was bound to be revenge in his mind for the death of his brother. Baruch hadn't fired the shotgun, but Abel would want to kill Baruch for what had happened. It put a big strain on Baruch's mind and the journey was about to cross too much unin-habited country with endless opportunities for ambush. When he had set out on his own, he was confident that he could look out for himself. Now with two bodies, one of which was very much alive, it was a whole different matter. Worse still, he couldn't put that gold ring out of his mind. There was no doubt it belonged to his pa.

Spurring his horse into a quick trot, Baruch had a premonition that it would not be long before the first test of his mettle. He was not wrong.

3

They hadn't ridden more than a couple of hours before Abel Benson was calling for water. The sun was beating down from a clear blue sky, and Baruch was sure this would be the first of many opportunities that Benson was going to try and turn to his advantage.

'You don't need no water yet,' Baruch said shaking his head. 'We ain't stopping till I say so, so just hush up.'

Abel spat to the side of his horse. 'I'm parched dry as a desert, didn't get no breakfast, and if you want me to treat you good when I manage to git free you'd better be nice to me, boy.'

It was a disconcerting threat. The possibility of his prisoner getting free was on Baruch's mind anyway. He didn't need a warning to make the situation any worse. It wasn't the only worry that was going through his mind. There was the irrefutable evidence of his pa's ring that he found in a box in one of the saddle-bags. Some of the jewellery also seemed familiar. It was all adding up to evidence that this man, Abel Benson or his dead brother, Kane, had somehow been involved in the ransacking and torching of his parents' shebang. Unless they had traded bounty with Erik Elias, and were innocent of any connection with the criminal activity in Vendigo, Baruch had unwittingly caught two of the perpetrators. This put added pressure on him to bring Abel Benson to justice.

'You don't think you're going to get me to any jailhouse, do yer?' Abel shouted out from the trailing horse roped to Baruch's saddle horn. 'That's certain, cos I got friends out here, y'know.'

Baruch made no reply. He didn't want to engage in conversation: he was too intent scouring the countryside with his eyes, seeking out telltale dust rising on the road or flashes of sunlight from the barrels of rifles. He had the unnerving feeling that he was being watched. It was inevitable that the hair on his neck should tingle from time to time; it was the nature of the task to be constantly worried.

About ten miles away from Radford, they came across their first traveller, going in the opposite direction. It was an old-timer, a trader on a pony with a couple of mules laden with goods under a cloth cover. As Baruch drew level, the man looked surprised at the sight of the prisoner with bound hands. He raised his hat.

'Say, you got a prisoner, boy?'

'Sure thing, mister.'

'D'you need any help?' the trader asked.

'Such as?'

'Well, I can see a load of flies buzzing round that tarp, so I guess you got a dead'un there, too. You a bounty hunter?'

'No, sir, that I am not. Just an ordinary citizen bringing a man to justice.'

The trader scratched at his stubbly chin. He was chewing a wad of tobacco that he swirled round in his mouth, making a loud sucking noise as he bared his yellow front teeth – all five of them. 'Where you headin', west to Vendigo or north to Maple Cross?'

Baruch was wondering what sort of help this little wizened old man could possibly offer. His face was weather-beaten, coloured and wrinkled like the shell of a walnut. At least he didn't look like much of a threat, and he wasn't carrying any gun that Baruch could see.

'I'm on my way to Vendigo,' Baruch said.

'Bad choice,' the man replied. 'Sheriff there is a no-good lawman. If I was you I'd head north to Maple Cross. They got a marshal there right now, he's the one you should see.'

Baruch was alarmed at this news. 'What d'you know about the sheriff at Vendigo Bluff? Who says he's a bad lawman?'

'I do. Sheriff's name is Greg Hempson. I heard he used to be on the other side of the law until he found he could run his business without fear of capture by being an elected lawman.'

'That's pretty strong words.'

'I don't go near Vendigo these days, only go east to west with a diversion to Maple Cross – that's where I've just come from.'

Baruch had little choice but to go to Vendigo, since that's where his parents were and that was the original purpose of his journey. He didn't want the encumbrance of a prisoner and his dead brother, but now suspecting they were something to do with the crime, he was glad to be taking them to face justice – one of them, anyway.

The trader squeezed his heels into his pony. 'Can't stop here jawing all day. Take my advice, son, and go north.'

The man rode on with his mules while Baruch commanded his horse into a quick trot. It was worrying. The trader didn't seem like a huckster, seemed an honest fellow, but the warning hadn't been missed. If the sheriff at Vendigo were crooked, there would be no hope of bringing Abel Benson to justice. It might even be dangerous to take him there. Suppose the sheriff was somehow involved with the Benson brothers? According to Jake, who brought the message, the sheriff hadn't been much use to his parents and had just stood by and watched while other folk helped as best they could. It was beginning to add up to a more dangerous endeavour than he could have imagined.

'Don't you worry 'bout that old fool,' Abel advised. 'Sheriff Hempson is a good man, he ain't nivver done no wrong.'

Words that were supposed to calm Baruch had

completely the opposite effect and simply strengthened the truth of what the trader had said. This gave Baruch a dilemma. A marshal in Maple Cross would certainly be a better bet than a crooked lawman in Vendigo where his parents were waiting for his help. Maple Cross was a good three days' ride.

He continued going west; he wouldn't have to make up his mind for a few more miles yet, not until he hit the north road at Mercer's Hole. A decision could wait.

It was time for a stop. He needed to think things through. He turned the horses off the road and into the scrub. He slid down and dropped the reins over the horse's head. He had to hobble the other horse, as he didn't know if it might make a run. He warned Abel not try any funny business or he'd get a bullet, reminding him that, according to the dodger, he was wanted dead or alive. He sat him down roughly and roped his legs together, then gave him a water bottle. Tied hands didn't prevent him holding that.

Baruch gathered up some brushwood, placed a mug of water at the edge and set the fire alight. He sat down and waited for it to heat the water. With so many things running through his brain, he hardly knew when he was crushing coffee beans, chucking them into the water, lifting the mug out of the fire with two sticks, and putting on a riding glove to hold it. The coffee appeared in his hand almost by magic. But in that time he'd come to a decision.

Vendigo was where he had to get. His parents needed his help and furthermore there was clearly much more to this crime than just a family feud. If the sheriff were corrupt he'd have to cross that bridge when he came to it. Right now he needed to get to Vendigo as soon as possible. Without riding through the night it would be, at the very least, another day.

As Baruch kicked out the fire and packed up his things, Abel Benson couldn't resist taunting.

'You decided yet, sonny? Takin' me to the marshal at Maple Cross? Or my old pal Hempson at Vendigo?'

'Listen, Benson, I'd advise you to keep your mouth shut, or I might just dump you by the road and send word to the marshal to come and get you.'

'Dah, you'd nivver do that. You're soft as a milk jelly. You know I'd die of thirst out here.'

'Benson, the only reason I'm not leaving you here is exactly because you might die of thirst, and that wouldn't serve justice.'

Benson spat in the sand. 'Look, son, that dodger you found. That ain't a right thing. We nivver did no harm to nobody. Framed. That's what.'

'The dodger said you're wanted for robbery in Colorado, Arizona territory and Utah. It can't all be lies. And what about all that money and the box of jewellery? Anyways, that's for a judge to decide, not me.'

Baruch got the show on the road. Surprisingly Benson hadn't made any more comments, and even mounted up with a minimum of assistance. Baruch thought his words had at last won the day. It was a foolish complacency.

Ahead, the road swung round an outcrop and dropped down into a small canyon – not a deep one, but one with well-wooded slopes down to the trickle of a river at the sandy bottom where soft green willows lined the banks. When the river was this low it could be crossed by a ford marked out with a few tall poles. Middling height and the posts marked the crossing, but when it was in full flood a long diversion was necessary. It was a good watering hole for wildlife. Swathes of manzanita covered large patches of the rocky canyon sides with the verdant green glow of its strangely upright leaves dangling its little apple-like fruits. Birds were flittering around the trees, their song a welcome interlude to the near silence of the dusty desert.

For some unknown reason Baruch hesitated to descend to the river. He had an uneasy feeling that something was hiding in the tangle of bushes. He pulled the Winchester out of its holster and scrutinized every inch of ground. He fired a shot into the bank. All the birds rose up like an explosion of lead shot and then descended in their own flight pattern, as in the aftermath of a firework. In a moment all was settled. Satisfied that no puma or other dangerous animal was lurking by the bushes, Baruch spurred his horse slowly down the slope to the crossing place.

As he approached the river, the surface of the road softened and was pitted with horseshoe indentations and old wheel tracks. Water had gathered in some of the horseshoe dents, suggesting a rider had been through recently, as the water hadn't yet drained away. It was easy to see the old-timer's pony and mule tracks. But Baruch was interested in another set of prints that had recently crossed the river in the same direction that he was travelling, and yet he hadn't seen any sign of a rider up ahead.

The puzzle was soon solved. As Baruch rode up the other side of the canyon a rider appeared on the road at the top of the slope.

'Howdy, stranger,' the man said, holding up his hand in the acknowledged gesture to show he wasn't holding a gun. 'Need any help with your prisoner?'

It seemed everyone was keen to help him, even though he wasn't asking or indeed looking for any help. But this rider was nothing like the old trader with his mules. This man looked like trouble. Baruch could see at a glance that he was carrying two side arms, a sure sign of an outlaw or a lawman, and there wasn't any badge in evidence. He was clean-shaven, rugged and weather-beaten, with a firm jaw, a scar on his left cheek and piercing blue eyes.

The man continued to smile at Baruch. 'I heard a gunshot and thought I'd take a look. Was that you?'

'Yes, it was. Flushing out the wildlife, just in case.'

'Very wise,' the man agreed. Then he looked more closely at the prisoner. 'Well I be darned if that ain't Abel Benson. How you doing, Abe? Not too good by the look of it.' He threw his head back and laughed.

'You know this man?' Baruch said to the rider.

'Sure I know this man. He's my brother.'

'Another one?'

'Another one?' the man repeated pulling his six-gun. 'There ain't no more of us, sonny. Just the two of us. . . .' He fired a shot into the air.

Baruch was mystified. 'But. . . .'

Kane Benson was still smiling at Baruch as he got down off his horse and walked down the slope. 'You done a good job, boy. See, my brother Abel here and that low-down Morgan ran out on me with all my cash.' He went up to Abel and looked him in the eye. 'Didn't work out, did it?'

Baruch was tempted to pull his handgun, but thought better of it. It wasn't at all clear how this scenario would play out.

Kane turned back to Baruch. 'Who's in the tarp? Is that Morgan you got there?'

'Guess so,' Baruch replied. 'If he was with your brother this morning, than that's his body in the tarp.'

Kane slapped his thigh. 'Well, good riddance. Now we got to decide what to do with my little brother here.'

Baruch was too bold. 'I'm taking him to Vendigo to claim the reward on the dodger that was in Morgan's slicker.'

'Might as well whistle in the wind, sonny. Hempson ain't no use, he won't give you a penny piece for my brother.'

This news was somewhat deflating. Baruch had to

think quickly. Bryce Radford had all the cash and the jewellery box. If Kane found out about that, he'd be bound to go and demand his cash. That would put Radford and Mary-Lou in great danger.

'There wasn't any cash,' Baruch declared. 'We searched the saddle-bags and found a few bits of jewellery, but no cash.'

Kane looked at Abel. 'No cash? Where'd you hide that?'

'It was in the saddle-bags, I swear it.'

Kane spat. 'Now look you here, Abe. Who am I goin' to believe? This honest young man taking you to justice because that's what the law says, or a snivelling runaway who stole my cash and ran out on me?'

'They took the money, Kane.'

'Who?'

'This boy and the saloon owner, the one who shot Morgan.'

Baruch wanted to bring this to an end before something sparked off. Kane Benson was likely to be a ruthless individual when he was roused and this matter of the cash was clearly beginning to get to him. Baruch figured Bryce wouldn't be upset at the loss of a thousand dollars for the reward; he had all the dollars out of the saddle-bag after all. He settled on a plan.

'I could just hand him over to you,' Baruch said to ease the tension. 'You can take him. And Morgan's body.'

'Mebbe, son, mebbe.'

Kane walked around for a bit, kicking up the dust with his boot. He was clearly deep in thought. He kept twirling his gun round in his hand. This was not a man to mess with and Baruch wanted to be on his way. If only Kane would relieve him of Abel and the body, everything would be good. Except the money . . . he had a feeling Kane wasn't going to let that go.

'Tell you what,' he said to Baruch. 'I'll take Abe and Morgan, and you'll swear to me there was no money in those saddle-bags. But if there was, and I found out you lied, you're a dead man, d'you understand?'

'Yes,' said Baruch. 'The saddle-bags were near empty.'

'Right. Give me the horses and I'll take these two off your hands.'

Baruch was mightily relieved. He wanted to know what Kane planned to do with his brother but instinct told him to get away from this situation as fast as he could. He dismounted, untied the rope that was securing the horses and handed them to Kane Benson.

'Over to you.'

Kane levelled his gun. 'It sure is, sonny. So untie that gunbelt and drop it on the ground.'

'What?'

'The gunbelt, drop it.' Kane Benson was waving his six-gun nonchalantly. 'And is that a Winchester, on the saddle? I'll have that too.'

This was exactly what Baruch feared would

happen. He went to take the rifle out of the scabbard.

'That's all right where it is,' Kane said. 'Leave it
there. I'll take it with the horse.'

Baruch was being robbed. But that wasn't the
worst of it. He watched Kane cut the rope on Abel's
hands and let him slide down off the horse. They
smiled and embraced.

Abel spoke first. 'Good to see you, brother. I was
getting worried. Thought this greenhorn might take
me to Maple Cross.'

Kane shook his head. 'You shouldn't doubt me.
I've been riding alongside from Radford. Figured
you and Morgan had run into a spot of bother in the
saloon. What happened to Morgan?'

'Barkeep shot him. Morgan tried to draw on him.
I suggest we get this boy to bury him here in the
sand.'

'Good idea. You hear that, son? Fetch my knife
from the saddle and cut yourself a stick to dig with.'

Baruch was very frightened. Like everybody else
in these parts he'd heard of people having to dig
their own grave before being robbed and killed.
Kane showed him where to dig downriver away from
the crossing. The ground was mercifully soft but it
still took him an age to dig a shallow grave big
enough to take Morgan's body. It was with great
relief that he unwrapped the tarp and laid the body
in the grave.

'Now you can take it nice and easy, son,' Kane
said. 'Keep the tarp, you might need it for shelter.'

He turned to Abel. 'You got anything to say to this boy?'

'Might have,' Abel replied walking over to Baruch. 'No hard feelings?' He held out his hand to Baruch. Baruch went to shake Abel's hand, but Abel's fist flashed up under his chin fast as lightning, and the world went completely black.

4

The world was at an odd angle and very blurred. A bright light was shining in his eyes. It cleared gradually, the light faded and everything began to assume proper shapes with distinct outlines and colours that were not so bright. It was not the first time Baruch had been knocked unconscious, but it was the first time he'd been laid out as an adult. His chin was sore. He ran his hand around his jaw. Painful but not broken. The blow had evidently connected with a blood vessel, shutting off supply to the brain for a second. His body corrected the situation by falling down so blood could flow freely again. Coming round was a strange sensation of disorientation. The world seemed like a place he had never been in before, then everything fell into place and life resumed where it left off. Almost.

He got to his knees, still a bit shaky. Reality was beginning to kick in. The Bensons had taken everything: his horse, his guns and his water. The tarp lay on the ground, a reminder of how the day had started. Then he thought of Morgan. Was there still a gun in the holster when he'd buried him? The Bensons hadn't been too bothered about the body, they'd just watched from a distance when he had been digging. He'd just undone the tarp and rolled the body into the grave. It was worth a look.

He searched for the digging stick that he had discarded and began the gruesome task of scooping the sand with his hands to exhume the body. It reminded him that one never knows what people will do when the need arises. He would never have thought he'd be burying a body in the sand, let alone digging it up again. It seemed in every way sacrilegious, but had to be done.

It did not take long to get to the sandy corpse. Baruch had to set aside the distasteful aspect of what he was doing. At last he was rewarded. The slicker had protected the gunbelt, bullets and six-gun from most of the sandy mud. He undid the belt. Yanking and twisting he was able to release the belt and pull it out of the grave. Covering the body for a second time took a lot more effort. But at the end of the operation he had a gun and a handful of bullets.

He wiped the gun and began to take it apart. It was a heavy Colt rimfire with a long barrel and an ivory grip, a powerful weapon and the kind favoured by outlaws for delivering a heavy punch over a long distance. Having cleaned it up as much as he could he prepared to fire a test shot. Holding the gun well away from his body, he turned his head away and then had second thoughts. The noise would carry for miles: much too risky after the last episode. If he was threatened by a wild animal or more outlaws he'd just have to hope it fired properly.

He rolled the tarp as small as possible; it was the only thing the Bensons had left him. It was cumbersome, but faced with the prospect of a night in the desert and the drop in temperature, he was glad to carry it. Trying to put the best face on things, he set off on the road out of the canyon and prayed that a passing horseman, trader or even an outlaw might give him a ride to the next small cluster of buildings. He knew there was a small town called Mercer's Hole where the road to Maple Cross went north, but he wasn't sure how far away it was. He resigned himself to a long walk.

Some people are lucky and some are not. Some have a complicated mixture of both good and bad luck, and so it was with Baruch. Having had some very bad luck being taken in by the Bensons, a piece of good luck was about to come his way. He'd been properly duped by Kane Benson pretending he was angry with his brother, Abel, when in fact quite the opposite was the case and he was playing a clever game. Once he had lulled Baruch into a false sense of security, Kane pulled his gun, and Baruch's bad luck followed from that.

But now Baruch could hear the faint jingle of horse trappings and the rumble of a wheeled wagon. There was hardly any cover for him to hide behind and the contraption was, by the sound of it, crossing the canyon and about to emerge on this side. Baruch had no alternative but to stand his ground and await its arrival. He stepped to the side of the road and stood casually to face up. He put his hands up in a gesture seeking assistance, palms open, fingers splayed, a little like surrendering, but his muscles were taught and his right hand was ready to drop below the holster for a rapid upward draw should the need arise. It didn't: the wagon came to a stop and the driver called down.

'Looking for a ride?'

'I sure am,' Baruch replied, his eyes lighting up.

'What you got in the tarp?'

Baruch looked at the bundle of folded cloth that was at his feet. 'Nothing. You can have it, if you like. I need a ride to Mercer's Hole, or further if you're going west.'

'All the way to the Navajo reservation,' was the reply.

This was good news. 'By way of Vendigo Bluff?'

'Yep. All these goods is for the Indians.' He gestured behind him at the wagon.

Baruch looked at the ramshackle affair like a wagon from a travelling circus. The cart was high-sided, roofed, painted dull green and probably served both as accommodation and freight carrier. It had more than likely started out as a very smart piece of travelling kit.

'Don't look much, do it?' the driver said. 'But it does the job. Name's Clive Bootle. What's yours?'

'Baruch Elias.'

'Elias? Same as the shebang at Vendigo?'

'Yes, sir, that's my parents' store.' He quickly corrected himself, 'Was.'

'Was? Come on, jump up. Let's keep movin'. I usually stock up there in Vendigo. What's happened?'

Baruch climbed up to share the wooden seat with Clive Bootle, and over the next half-dozen miles relayed the story of the attack on the store in Vendigo as told him by Jake out at the Sigurrson ranch. Then he explained his very recent encounter with the Benson brothers that had left him robbed and without a horse.

At the end of it, Clive turned sideways and looked Baruch in the eye. 'Do I see revenge in that face?'

Baruch hesitated. 'I don't know what I feel. I'm pretty sore about the Bensons, and I know they had something to do with the attack on the store. And I guess I'm a bit shook up about my folks. But until I get to the truth of what happened, I don't rightly know what I'm going to do.'

The conversation lapsed into silence, as both men were deep in their own thoughts. As the workhorse plodded on along the track, the gentle swaying of the wagon was soporific. A couple of times Baruch began dozing. The third time it happened, Clive Bootle woke him up with a suggestion.

'Listen, fella, you don't want to be going at this pace. You probably noticed I got a pony hitched at the back of the wagon. Why don't you borrow her and ride yourself on to Mercer's Hole? You'll be there long before me. You can leave the pony at the

48

livery and hire yourself something fast to get to Vendigo. What do you say?'

Baruch didn't reply immediately; a crazy thought was rushing through his head and heating his blood. It was a long shot but the best plan he could come up with.

'You're right,' he said suddenly to Clive. 'It's a generous offer and I'll gladly accept. And another thing you're right about: you did see revenge in my eyes.'

Within a few moments, Baruch had descended the wagon, unhitched the pretty little chestnut pony, taken the saddle off the back of the wagon and placed it over the saddlecloth. He attached the bridle and reins, stroking the muzzle as he did so to calm the pony, adjusted the stirrups, tightened the cinch and mounted up. He drew level with Clive waiting patiently on the driver's seat. Clive had taken the opportunity of a stop to undo his tobacco pouch and squeeze himself a plug. Baruch watched him roll it round between his fingers and push it up between his teeth and gums. He swirled some saliva round and made a loud sucking noise before spitting into the sand.

'Now don't you worry 'bout Sally, she'll be fine.'
'Sally?'
'The hoss. You leave her at Mercer's Hole and I'll collect her later.'

'I won't forget your kindness,' Baruch said, urging Sally into a gentle trot. He waved his arm in farewell, and was surprised at the speed with which the pony wanted to go. Perhaps being tied up behind a slow old cart wasn't Sally's idea of fun. Never mind what the pony was thinking, there was just one mission consuming Baruch. Although several miles adrift, he was now on the trail of the Benson brothers and sooner or later he'd catch up with them. As it happened, it was to be sooner rather than later.

Sally had boundless energy. Undoubtedly used to the relatively slender weight and frame of Clive Bootle, the pony didn't seem at all perturbed by the size or weight of her new rider. If anything, it seemed to give her extra pleasure to feel a proper horseman on the other end of her reins. The miles were consumed effortlessly and Mercer's Hole eventually came into view. It was mid-afternoon, but distances are very deceptive in the desert, and what may look a half hour's ride away may take a couple of hours to cover in reality.

So it was with Baruch's first view of the little township. He was well aware of desert distances and the tricks light and shadows can play, so he wasn't surprised when the sun was much lower in the sky by the time he rode into town. He hadn't originally planned on stopping at Mercer's Hole. With proper progress he would by now have been close to Vendigo with just this night's stop. But with everything that had happened, he was still maybe two days' ride away.

Instead of riding into the livery yard, he hitched outside the town's one saloon, a single storey, garishly-painted brick building in a street of otherwise mostly timber frame construction without false fronts. The saloon was probably the one solid building in the whole area. He opened the door and walked in, expecting the room to fall silent and all eyes to swivel. Strangely, nothing like that happened. There was plenty of noise from the several pokes gathered around the faro table and chat, smoke and clinking glasses filled the rest of the room. The room itself was far too big for the town, and there was even a stage at the far end. Heaven knows when the town would ever attract a troupe of dancers. Maybe the local folk took it in turns to entertain for an evening.

The barkeep engaged Baruch's attention with a nod of the head in place of any words. Baruch responded in similar manner.

'Glass of beer, please,' he added, conscious that he was hot and sweaty from the hard ride. But there was no time to lose. He drank half the glass in one gulp, wiped his mouth on his sleeve and eyeballed the barkeep.

'Have you had a couple ridge riders in here today, around midday perhaps, laughing and joking? They're brothers. Pulling an extra horse, a fine-looking quarter horse, black with white socks on its front legs?'

'Don't know about white socks, but I do know about brothers,' the man said.

'Brothers?'

'Yessir, they were brothers all right and proud of it. Came right in, ordered drinks, and when they spoke they called each other brother. So I guess they were.'

'How long ago?'

'Few hours.'

'They'll have a good lead on me by now.'

The barkeep shook his head. 'Another beer? They won't have got far, drinking for a while here; they left about an hour ago. Maple Cross direction, I think.'

'Gee, that's real good news.' Baruch went to pay and then realized he hadn't got any money. 'Listen, they robbed me this morning. Can you chalk my beer and I'll pay on my way back.'

The barkeep gave Baruch a long, hard stare, and then he smiled. 'Reckon so. Lucky you've got an honest face.'

Baruch thanked him profusely and was just about to go out of the door when he suddenly realized the room was completely silent and everyone was staring at him. He stopped in his tracks, hand on the door handle and looked at the blank faces.

They'd all been listening. Someone, somewhere, spoke in a slow drawl. 'Good luck, son . . . They was the Benson brothers. Drinks on me if you come back alive.'

Baruch touched his hat in recognition of the warning. He wished he'd heard that earlier in the day. Once outside, he unhitched the pony and leapt into the saddle.

'Now, Sal, we've got a helluva ride. I hope you're up to it. You've got to go like the wind.'

He turned the pony onto a road where there was a fingerboard scratched with the name Maple Cross, the letters blackened with a hot poker. He kicked his spurs into the pony's flanks and was soon at full gallop. Figuring the Bensons were probably not in any hurry, he reckoned half an hour of fast riding might just get them in sight before dusk.

So after more than three quarters of an hour and no sign of them, he decided they had either galloped on and were much further ahead, or they had turned off the track to find somewhere to camp out for the night. It was a toss up. He decided in view of their time spent drinking they wouldn't be galloping anywhere. Most likely they had turned off the track to camp, but where?

The sun was descending behind the hills in the west, and soon it would be impossible to find any trace of the two riders. Disconsolately, he turned the pony back in the direction they had just ridden. Sally was a game little pony, and although her flanks were heaving and there was dribble and flecks of saliva round her mouth, Baruch knew she was good for more riding. Now at a steady, gentle trot, they retraced their steps slowly because Baruch was studying the ground as they passed over it. He flicked his eyes left and right, looking for a break in the scrubby vegetation where riders might have left the road. In the east, away to his left, the mountainous ground rose rapidly into a series of high ridges. On the steep face there were many nooks and crannies, perfect for hideouts and lookouts, but too far away to merit the ride for a campsite. Maybe they had started a fire to cook some supper; smoke would be real helpful right now.

Finding any trace of the Bensons would have been impossible: searching for a campsite could have taken hours and revealed nothing. A line of smoke drifting up to the sky would have been best, but second best after sight is sound – the sound of gunshots carries very clearly across the desert. So Baruch's heart leapt when suddenly . . . *Bang! Bang!* Two such gunshots enabled him to get a clue on the direction, and then another two were fired in such a similar way that it was almost certainly a signal of some sort. Alerted by the first two shots, when the second two were fired Baruch had a fix on a very precise location. Peering in that direction, he sighted a clump of trees taller than anything else. It would serve as a waymark.

'Now then, Sally, old girl,' he said, despite the likelihood that the pony wasn't above five years old, 'I think we just found the Bensons. So we have to go nice and gentle, slow and stealthy.' He leant forward and affectionately pulled an ear.

He talked the pony into a slow trot and, turning off the road, began to pick his way over the stony ground through the low scrub, avoiding the sharp spines of the cholla and cactus. The hills began to rise a little less than a half mile away, and as they got nearer it was obvious there was a watercourse running beside the cliff face. The vegetation changed to a low growth of juniper and, where there was enough groundwater, the willow and cottonwood clump.

He decided this was the place to dismount and continue on foot. He hitched the pony in the cover of the vegetation and started to explore the watercourse. He began searching for fresh tracks in the wet sand. It took less than ten minutes to find the crossing place, but there was a surprise in store. The number of shoed hoof prints suggested that more riders than just the Bensons had recently crossed this way. It wasn't easy to be sure but it looked like at least five tracks. If the Bensons crossed here with Baruch's stolen horse, then at least two other riders were already here. Baruch was beginning to think this was something more permanent than an overnight stop-off.

After another hundred yards of creeping through the cover, the unmistakeable smell of horses was drifting in the air. He was now less than fifty yards from the rock face. This was undoubtedly a camp but there was no sound of voices. Crawling slowly through the long creosote fronds and stunted juniper, he could see a line of horses hitched at a rail, six in total. He was careful not to make any sudden movements and disturb any birds that might raise an alarm call. Soon, all became clear. There was a makeshift enclosure of wooden posts and brushwood, just enough to form a boundary for the horses. Beyond the line of tethered animals was a good-sized hole in the rock face. Whoever was here was inside some kind of cave. What a perfect hideout.

Baruch laid low. He could see Whitey tethered

with the others. The saddles hadn't been removed from his horse, or the two that the Bensons had been riding, so they had not long arrived at this place. It showed they cared little for anything. Any decent horseman would have removed the saddles straight away – unless, of course, they were planning to move out quite soon.

Suddenly there was movement at the entrance to the cave. A woman came out. This was a huge surprise. She went over to the horses, removed the saddles from the Bensons' mounts and unhitched them all. She talked to them in turn except Whitey. They snorted, shook their heads and wandered around in the enclosure. She left the saddle and everything on Whitey; he was well laden with the bedroll, saddle-bags and the Winchester still in the scabbard.

Perhaps the woman had been told to leave it, or maybe she couldn't be bothered to unload it, or maybe she didn't care about a horse that didn't belong to them. Whatever the reason, it made Baruch think hard about his next move. It was certainly time to move: something with a lot of very small legs was crawling up his arm. Looking at the ground he could see insects taking advantage of the last of the sun's warmth to do whatever they had to do. It would soon be dark.

So, it was evident that with saddles removed, nobody was going anywhere. At least three people were here, the Bensons and the woman, but who else? It crossed Baruch's mind that this might be the hideout for the whole gang including his uncle, Erik Elias. He hated to think of that man as his uncle. How could someone attack their own brother, destroy their store and livelihood and leave them traumatised and injured? What sort of a man was Erik Elias? Baruch had never met him, or couldn't remember doing so. What could have sparked off such hatred?

If this was their hideout, it was far too dangerous for Baruch to do anything. He would be sure to end up like Morgan in a shallow grave, and he didn't fancy the prospect. Maybe one of the horses was Morgan's, so that was one spare horse without a rider. Maybe there were only four people here, Erik Elias, the Benson brothers and the woman.

It was still too dangerous to attempt anything, but there was one thing he didn't want to leave behind, and that was Whitey. His plan now was to wait until dark. It was highly unlikely they'd put a guard on the horses. There was no need. Nobody knew they were here, or so they thought. All this was in Baruch's favour; all he had to do was wait until dark. He found himself a better vantage point to study the exact layout of the cave entrance, the hitching rail, the enclosure and its makeshift gate.

At last, dusk fell, quickly followed by darkness, then the chill air of a desert night began to swirl.

There was just one question on Baruch's mind: how to get his horse without it looking like someone had taken it. There was only one answer: to make it look like the horses had broken out, and that would be very difficult to manage. Nevertheless, it had to be done.

5

The desert is rarely pitch black. A clear sky dotted with myriad stars gives at least enough light to make out some larger shapes, like horses. That night was even better with a big silver moon reflecting light from the other side of the world. The edge of the enclosure was clear enough, the horses were clear enough, the entrance to the cave was clear enough. Could he risk taking some steps towards the entrance and listen, or even try to see what was inside? The faintest flickering glow of orange light suggested that the cave was deep, and that there was some kind of lantern and undoubtedly a fire some-where deep inside the rock.

Baruch's heart was beating fast. It was time for action before the cold night air made his muscles less flexible and cramped up his legs. He steeled himself: it was now or never. He crept through the last bit of cover, slipped through the brushwood fence and approached the entrance to the jagged fissure in the rock. He could hear his heart: *thump, thump, thump.* He eased his way along the rock face, straining his ears for any sound of voices. He prayed that the horses would make no fuss; he was conscious that with their night vision they could see his shadowy figure creeping about.

It was too late to worry about footprints since there were bound to be plenty already, and hoof marks would be everywhere as well. He edged closer to the opening and took a couple of steps into the tunnel. He trod carefully, wary of slipping on loose stones or making a sudden noise.

Some twenty yards in, he could hear voices and then a short burst of music on a mouth organ, followed by laughter. Would he dare go in any further? Another turn in the tunnel might be irreversible. Or there might even be a tripwire attached to empty tin cans. But curiosity is a powerful force, and against his better judgement Baruch eased his way forward step at a time. Another turn in the tunnel with a roof so low he had to stoop for a dozen yards before coming to a spot where he was surprised that he could hear voices.

Being still and cavernous, speech was being distorted by the strange acoustics. It was impossible to tell who was speaking, but there seemed to be three male voices. Parts of the conversation were quite clear, and other parts were difficult to discern over the cracking of the firewood; it must have been the woman playing the mouth organ that overrode the talk.

'It's a shame Morgan isn't here to join us . . . fault . . . draw.'

'God rest his soul.'

'That boy . . . pay for it . . . if we. . . .'

'It . . . barkeep. . . .'

'Don't matter who . . . Listen, you two, I sent you . . . Vimy . . . Sigurrson ranch. I have . . . settle. So . . . doing what I told you, you end up in a brawl in some two-bit town . . . Morgan . . . blown away. Can't I trust you to do. . . .'

'It was . . . luck.'

'Gee boss, we didn't . . . turn out . . . wanted some breakfast.'

'Of course you knew . . . pair of hotheads like you . . . weren't you in there?'

'It's a good thing I wasn't or I . . . rescue Abel.'

'So who was . . . you left out . . . a bounty hunter? Why didn't you kill him?'

'. . . just a boy . . . he might have died of thirst anyway.'

'So tomorrow . . . again, and this time . . . the Sigurrson ranch . . . don't ask directly . . . see if the name gets mentioned.'

The mouth organ stopped. There was a short pause. 'Supper's ready now, boys.'

Baruch had heard enough. It was time to make himself scarce. He retraced his steps. Whitey was what he wanted, that was all that mattered at this moment.

Coming back out into the dark of the night, Baruch let out a stream of breath like a long sigh. He hadn't realized that he'd been holding back, hardly daring to breathe inside the cave. Now, somehow, he had to get his horse out of the enclosure and ride off, then find the trader's pony and get clean away from the hideout.

He now realized it would have been good to use the noise of the mouth organ in the cave to cover any noise of removing his horse. What he had heard had been worth the risk, though: what sort of business had these men got to do with Arnie Sigurrson? Arnie was as straight as a die; he wouldn't have business with people like the Bensons, surely? Perhaps he should ride back to the ranch to warn Arnie, or should he go on to Vendigo?

The immediate problem was to make the removal of his horse look like a natural happening by opening the gate and hoping it would appear to have blown open in the night. With any luck the other horses might wander out a short distance, although they would be unlikely to do so until the morning: none of them were hobbled. He just had to hope everyone in the cave slept late and came out to find their horses wandering about outside the enclosure eating whatever they fancied.

Too much thought is not a good thing. Baruch approached Whitey and quickly stroked the muzzle in a kind of *keep quiet* gesture. The horse pricked its ears in response. The gate was freestanding, staying where it was only by the force of its own weight. This was good. He pushed the gate just far enough to lead his horse through. He paused a moment to see

if any of the others felt inclined to follow. One whin-
nied and the rest stood looking, their eyes glinting
in the moonlight. Baruch quickly led Whitey away
and went to find the tied pony. Helpfully, Sally
snorted as Baruch approached.

His heart still beating faster than normal, Baruch
roped Sal to his saddle horn, mounted up and rode
quietly back towards the track. Once away from the
rockface, he soon broke into a fast trot and then a
canter once his eyes were fully accustomed to the
moonlit road.

Light was still showing in the saloon windows at
Mercer's Hole when Baruch rode past. He was
tempted to stop and show them he was still alive,
claim the promised drink and pay the slate, but he
needed to put as much distance as possible between
that hideout and himself. He did, however, pull up
quietly at the livery and tie up Sally in the yard,
hanging the saddle on the fence and slipping the
bridle off. Someone would feed her in the morning
and the trader would be along to pick her up later.

Glad to have succeeded in retrieving his own
horse and kit, he wanted to press on to Vendigo. It
bothered him a lot that he couldn't warn Arnie, and
he was very concerned about Ingrid, but his first
duty was to his parents. Once he'd checked that they
were at least safe, he'd get back to Vimy Point and
the ranch as quickly as he could. He was determined
to ride through the night and with a bit of luck,
without running Whitey into the ground, he'd be in
Vendigo by end of the next day.

Riding at night was something of a new experience.

Of course he'd occasionally had to go out late to check on the cattle when the dogs had barked to warn of predatory animals. But riding along roads when they were silent and deserted felt eerie. The moonlight marked out the road like a ribbon of silver foil. Trees were no longer green, but mostly an ominous black with silvery-white tips where the moon touched their outline. Distant mountains were darker than the sky, except on their very ridges where the tops were delineated with a strong purple line edged in the light of the stars. Rodents scurried across the road occasionally, and every now and then the sudden black shape of an owl would swoop silently past his ears. Away in the distance, announcing a recent kill, he could hear the distinctive yapping howl of coyotes. A prairie dog ran across the road. This nocturnal world was almost another planet.

But the greatest show was yet to come, and the curtain began to rise around four o'clock in the morning when the dark night sky turned to a shade of Prussian blue, before gradually transforming into a wonderful arc of pure cerulean, into which the sun burst like a shower of gold. It was a spectacular sight, and how he wished Ingrid were by his side to share it with him.

Cold and hungry, it was a warming thought as he imagined her lovely blue eyes sparkling in the sunlight, and her mouth set in a disarming smile. How he longed to hold her in his arms. These warm thoughts carried him on for another couple of hours until he decided to stop and give Whitey a rest. He pulled off the road into a good cover of brushwood around a stand of ponderosa pine where he could gather enough fallen wood to light a small fire, just enough to boil some water and make coffee.

Sitting on an old fallen log, Baruch rolled himself a smoke and drank his mug of steaming hot coffee. Ahead of him lay a day of imagined horrors, a burnt out shebang, traumatised parents, an unhelpful sheriff. He wondered what all that would really be like. Could it be as bad as Jake had suggested? Whatever lay in store he was determined, God willing, to get to the bottom of this callous act and if necessary bring someone, all of them, to justice. At least he knew where the Bensons were hiding.

Just as he had hoped, it was the middle of the afternoon when he found himself riding into Vendigo Bluff. This was more than a two-bit town, and had grown even bigger in the four years that he'd been away. Vendigo was the hub of local commerce. Main Street's line of false fronts declared an aspiration. It was already a trade crossroads and an agricultural market, the largest settlement in that corner of Utah besides Maple Cross. It boasted hotels, saloons, a bank, a church, the whole range of stores and every kind of service from land agents and lawyers to the usual saddlers and a gunsmith. According to a sign on the Silver Cactus saloon, there was even a regular chorus line that danced every Friday and Saturday night. The Elias hardware store was the biggest trading business in town . . . or used to be.

For the last couple of miles the light westerly wind had carried a faint odour of burnt wood on the air. As he got closer to the town he realized it was the smouldering remains of his parents' thriving business, now a heap of charred timber and a virtually unrecognisable jumble of blackened stock. All that had survived the fire was a small group of stovepipes, metal items and the metal parts of things like tools, rolls of wire, bits of barrels, and that kind of thing. One wall built of brick, stood gaunt and black and in the middle of the ruin, looking forlorn and eerie, the store's own stovepipe that townsfolk used to sit round on cold winter days.

He didn't waste too much time looking at the smoking ruin. He rode on down Main Street to the sheriff's office, hitched outside and went in. Three men with badges were engaged in conversation, looking over a map.

'This would be the best place,' one of them said.

'Sheriff Hempson?' Baruch asked.

The three men carried on studying the map, pointing to various trails, doing their best to ignore the intruder.

'There's a good pinch point here,' another said, jabbing the map with his finger.

'Sheriff Hempson,' Baruch repeated. 'I'm Baruch Elias and I want a word.'

At this second interruption, the three men

stopped what they were doing and turned to look at the young man who had broken up their conversation. Two of them remained standing. The third took a long cigar out of his top pocket, went to the drawer of his desk, took out a match, struck it and lit the cigar. He shut the drawer slowly and deliberately, then sat down in the chair and looked up.

'That's me, son. Who are you and what do you want?'

It was a rather brusque introduction, but Baruch was already on his guard remembering what the trader had told him about Hempson having been on the wrong side of the law and now a corrupt lawman. Jake had said Hempson did nothing to help his parents. Baruch decided to put his cards on the table.

'I told you, my name's Baruch Elias, I got a message that there'd been some trouble. I'm here to find out about the fire that destroyed my parents' store. Can I count on your help?' The question was deliberately shaped to put the sheriff on the spot.

'A right shame,' Hempson agreed with a twist of his head and down-turned eyes. 'Do what I can, son. Do what I can.' But he said this without looking directly at Baruch, and that was all the indication he needed to know which side the sheriff was on.

'Where are my parents now?'

'I guess with the Gillings. How did you hear about it?'

Baruch didn't want to give information. 'A messenger.'

'I guess it was their son, Jake, came to tell you.'

Baruch didn't bother to reply, but he noted that the sheriff was well informed. He went to the door. Just as he turned the handle, the sheriff said:

'I heard the doc say your pa might not live.'

Baruch couldn't stop himself looking over his shoulder. 'And what did you do to help them? I heard you just stood there watching.'

The sheriff didn't like Baruch's suggestion. He gave him a sly look but tried not to show any emotion. 'Nothin' we could do, son. Store was well alight, just made sure it didn't burn the town down.'

Baruch looked over the map that was spread out on a side table. The two deputies were leaning against the wall beside it.

Baruch whistled softly. 'Cattle trails? Well, what d'you know? I heard something about you and the wrong side of the law.'

With the first sign of annoyance, the sheriff blew out a stream of smoke with some force.

'Listen, son, take my advice. Leave the men to deal with men's business. You see to your folks then clear off out. Go back to wherever you came from and stay there. This ain't no place for boys.' He pointed to Baruch's handgun. 'And mind what you do with that. Any trouble, we shoot first and ask question afterwards.'

'That makes two of us,' Baruch retorted.

He closed the door firmly behind him, mounted up and watched for a moment. He heard a door close at the back of the sheriff's office. Then a deputy, mounted up, came out to the street and rode off at some speed. Baruch would like to have followed but his first task was to see his folk. He spurred his horse and set off in the opposite direction towards the Gillings' ranch.

6

Jake Gilling was a few years older than Baruch. He had occasionally helped out in the store and their parents had been good friends. It was no surprise that they had stepped in to look after Baruch's parents and that Jake had been the one to ride through day and night with the message. Now Baruch was afraid of what he might find at their ranch. Jake had said his pa was beaten up bad. But why? Why would his pa's brother, Erik, come out of jail and do a thing like that?

Deep in unsettling thoughts, it seemed the distance to the ranch was covered in no time. He rode under the gateway and down to the house. It was eerily quiet. He hitched at a rail and stepped onto the veranda, then knocked on the door and went in. His ma was sitting in a rocking chair, a shawl wrapped round her shoulders. She seemed to be asleep. Eveline Gilling, Jake's mother, went straight over to Baruch the moment he walked through the door. She put her hand on his chest to stop him approaching.

'Baruch. Oh, it's good to see you, boy. Don't wake your ma; I've finally got her to sleep. This is such a bad business.'

Baruch embraced Eveline and, while hugging her, thanked her quietly for what she was doing. 'Where's Pa?' he asked.

Eveline put her hand up and stroked his cheek. 'It's not good, Baruch. It's not good. He's here in one of our beds, but the doc isn't sure if he's going to pull through.'

'Can I see him?'

'Tomorrow. The doc was with him earlier and gave him some powders to make him sleep. Best not to disturb him. See him tomorrow.'

She steered him through the door and back out onto the veranda and towards a pair of old wicker-work chairs. They sat together.

Eveline was as puzzled as Baruch. 'I just don't understand it. Your pa's own brother. And just out of jail.'

'Was there something to do with him being locked up? Were my parents involved in that?'

'I don't know, boy. Whatever it is, they've lost their business and everything.'

They sat in silence for a while, neither quite knowing what to say next. It was Baruch who broke the spell.

'I heard the sheriff didn't do anything to help. Is

71

that true?'

'I don't trust the man,' Eveline said vehemently. 'Didn't raise a finger to do anything. Just watched the good folk form a chain of water buckets to stop the whole town burning down. An' he done nothin', not a darned thing.'

'Someone told me he used to be a cattle thief.'

'Wouldn't know 'bout that. Don't surprise me. You watch out for him. He's slippery as a damn catfish and twice as dangerous. Where you goin' to stay? We got room here. Let me get you some coffee.'

Baruch sat quietly on the veranda while Eveline went back inside. He was reflecting on his meeting with Sheriff Hempson and the deputy that rode off pretty quick out the back door.

Eveline brought out a tin mug of coffee. The sun had gone down and dusk was turning to nightfall.

'That's real kind. Look, I'm goin' back into town. Don't worry if I'm not back until late. I might stay around town to see what information I can pick up.'

'You know where the spare room is. I'll make up a bed for you. Take care, boy. If anything happened to you it might just finish off your ma and pa.'

Baruch mounted up and set off for town. He thought he would go to one of the several saloons and just join in the conversation. He'd be sure to be told things about the fire and, although not all rumours would be true, he might glean important information.

Vendigo was full of lively noise at night. Lanterns were hanging outside all the saloons and hotels, and the street was brightly lit. Music spilled out into the dust that was swirling with eddies of night air. Pianos, mouth organs, fiddles and the sound of boots dancing on wooden floorboards filled the spaces between the stores with their false fronts and garishly painted signs. Horses stomped occasionally at the rails as if listening to the music. People were strolling on the sidewalks to avoid the drunks wobbling along the street.

Baruch pushed through the batwings of one of the less noisy saloons and watched the card tables for a while. Dollars were clinking on the tables, and although there was plenty of shouting and loud talking it all seemed amicable enough. However, having been caught out once before, Baruch was carrying his side gun just in case. At least it was his own side gun retrieved from Whitey's saddle-bags. Retrieving his horse seemed so long ago, but it was only a matter of hours.

Eventually he went up to the bar and ordered a beer. He was soon chatting with a couple of local men who had been looking at him in an interested manner.

'Jes' passing thro'?' one of them asked.

'Here for a day or two,' Baruch replied. 'I was coming in for supplies but I heard there was a big fire in town. Burnt down the hardware shebang.'

'You must ha' seen it. On the corner. Elias place. Good folk, been here for years. Some crazy

73

horsemen on locoweed rode in and smashed them up, razed the place to the ground. What's yer name son?'

'Bar . . . Barclay,' he said hurriedly, thinking he'd get more information as a stranger just passing through.

'Good to meet you, Barclay. I'm Mart and this is my pardner, Tad.'

Baruch felt he'd alighted on a couple of locals who would have some information. They looked like farm hands but Mart was carrying a gun.

'Can I get you a drink? Have a beer on me.' Baruch called the barkeep over. 'Three beers when you're ready.'

'That's right civil of you,' Mart acknowledged.

The beers arrived.

'Your good health, Barclay,' Tad said, raising his glass.

'Did you know the horsemen?' Baruch ventured.

'No, never see'd 'em afore. But I heard they were friendly with Hempson.'

'You mean the sheriff?'

'Yes, but don't let him hear you talking 'bout it. He's not liked in town. Got a past, but we don't know exactly what.'

Baruch offered some knowledge. 'Cattle rustling, I think.'

'Where d'you hear that?' Tad asked.

'Keep yer voice down,' Mart warned.

'On the road. An old-timer told me to steer clear of Greg Hempson.'

'That figures.' The two men looked at each other and nodded in agreement.

Tad continued. 'Got himself elected by paying folk to vote for him. Now where did that money come from?'

Baruch pressed on. 'I was told he didn't lift a finger to help put out the fire.'

'Darned right he didn't. Folk were sayin' he had somethin' to do with it.'

'Did he?' Baruch asked.

Mart looked serious. 'You know, someone said the ringleader must've known Hempson, cos he went to see the sheriff before all the commotion.'

Tad nodded. 'There's a rumour going round the ringleader was Nils Elias's brother, Erik Elias. Just served time for murdering his wife. A family feud or something, but I don't know. . . .'

Mart interrupted. 'Good people, the Eliases. Can't run a town without people like that. Honest traders. We can do without bent lawmen, ain't no call for that. But that shebang is a big loss to the town. Someone'll set up, I guess.'

Baruch finished his beer and took his leave, shaking both men warmly by the hand before departing.

Outside, he breathed in deeply, feeling satisfied that he was on the right track. He leant back against the wall. It wasn't only Erik he had to worry about, the sheriff was somehow involved too, by the sound of it, and Baruch needed to find out just what that involvement was all about. It wasn't a coincidence they had been studying a map of the cattle trails and ranch boundaries when Baruch had walked into the office. Was Hempson involved in rustling?

It was time to make a move. Just as he stepped down off the boardwalk, a fight tumbled out of the saloon fifty yards down the road. Two men were rolling over in the dirt. Baruch stood and watched as people flocked round to see what was going on.

Then shots rang out and they ducked for cover. Baruch dodged behind a pillar. But the shots were nowhere near the fight. Two bullets zinged into the wall just behind Baruch and a third smashed into the wooden pillar. Splinters flew everywhere. He sank low to the floor and pulled his gun, straining his eyes to spot movement in the buildings opposite, he looked up and down the street. The fight had stopped. Was that just coincidence, or a carefully chosen opportunity?

One thing was sure: Baruch realized those three bullets were meant for him. Someone had been watching his movements and was waiting for him to come out of the saloon. Whoever it was, luckily, was a poor shot. But, beside Eveline Gilling and her husband, Jethro, was there someone else who knew who he was and that he was in town? The only answer to that was Hempson and his two deputies.

Baruch walked over to the sheriff's office immediately and went in. Hempson and the two deputies were chatting. This more or less proved that it wasn't one of them had just shot at him.

'Someone's just taken a couple of pot shots at me,' he said, going straight up to the sheriff who was sitting at his desk.

Hempson leant back in his chair. He pulled hard on his cigar while stroking his stubbly cheek.

'Guess this ain't no town for people poking around,' he said with a very unpleasant smile. 'This is a friendly town, son, so you must have upset someone.'

'Maybe even you?'

'Maybe.'

Baruch rode back to the Gilling ranch trying to figure out what he'd learnt. The moon was up and the stars were shining, shining as bright as the star on the sheriff's leather waistcoat. He was definitely one man to avoid, but would he really have tried to have him shot? He was tired. The last few days he had been high on adrenaline, and he was drained. It was with much relief that he rode into the Gillings' yard. It was late. Quietly he put his horse in the barn, removed the saddle, blanket and bridle and gave him some feed. Then he turned in for the night.

Sleep was a long time coming, and when it did it didn't last long enough. There was a dull grey light through the gap in the curtains. Baruch realized it was still nighttime. He drifted off into a fitful doze, dreaming of fire and people running with buckets of water. He was running too, and then he crashed into another person and woke abruptly. The grey light had become brighter. He got out of bed and pulled back the curtain. Eveline was sitting on the veranda, rocking slowly in her chair. Baruch dressed and went out to her.

'Guess you couldn't sleep, either,' Eveline said, getting up. 'You sit yourself down. I'll make you some hot coffee and boil some water for your shave. Everyone else is still asleep.'

Jethro came out and sat down beside Baruch.

'I'm just getting some coffee,' Eveline said to him.

Jethro nodded, then turned to Baruch. 'Sorry I didn't catch you last night, Baruch. You're very welcome. I'm glad you've come back; your folks need to see you, your pa especially. It might just give him the strength to pull through.'

Baruch was shaking his head. 'I'm glad Jake came to tell me. I just can't make head nor tail of why Pa's brother would do a thing like this.'

'Things in families run deep. Rivalries, jealousies, all that kind of bunkum. . . . You don't never know 'bout it till it all comes flooding out, especially with children. They all turn out different. We've been close to your parents for years and years, best of friends. We were married here in Vendigo and, like us your folks were devoted to each other. Jake was our first; he was a bit older than you. Your folks were going to have another baby but your ma miscarried and the doc said she couldn't have no more children after that.'

'But they did,' Baruch said. 'They had Ferdy, my brother.'

Jethro nodded. 'Yep, not long after the miscarriage, but something changed when they took in Ferdy.'

Baruch frowned. 'Took him in? What d'you mean, took him in? Ferdy's my brother. Was my brother. I don't like to talk about it really.'

'No, I guess not. And it's not my place to say nothing about it. But you didn't know?'

Eveline came out with the coffee. 'Water's ready if you want a shave, Baruch.'

All sorts of thoughts were racing through Baruch's mind. He couldn't believe what he had just heard. He didn't want to talk about Ferdy, but he couldn't leave it alone either.

'Eveline, Jethro just said Ferdy was taken in by my parents. What did he mean?'

Eveline looked at her husband and shook her head. 'That ain't for us to say, Jethro.' She turned to Baruch. 'I'd have thought you knew about Ferdy.'

'Only that I killed him.'

'No, you didn't, it was an accident.'

'But it was my fault.'

'You can't blame yourself, boy. Ferdy did what he did.'

'And died because of it. He was only eleven.'

Eveline sighed. 'Mebbe. But now the cat's out of the bag, I'll tell you what I know because your ma's too weak to spring this on her right now. But I guess you ought to know. You can't go on blaming yourself.'

Baruch began to sip his coffee. Conversation

came to a halt. The three of them sat in silence while the sun climbed into the sky to shed its light across the land. It was just such a light that might now be thrown across that horrendous incident from four years ago that had been swept under the carpet. That accident was the whole reason Baruch had left Vendigo to find a new life with the Sigurrsons at Vimy Point. Did he really want to know more about all that, and rake up such bad memories?

'I need to think about this. I'll have a shave.'

He went inside and took the kettle into his room. He poured the hot water into the basin, stropped his razor, lathered his face and scraped away the bristles. All the time he was thinking about Ferdy. About how they were always sparring, always competing. Ferdy could never win; he was eight years younger than Baruch and although Baruch would sometimes let him get the upper hand, the contests were never evenly matched. And then that dreadful day, the argument that should never have happened. Ferdy had pushed him too far and instead of holding onto him tightly Baruch had let him go. The stallion was angry and Ferdy, fired up with rage, was careless. It was all over so fast. Ferdy lying in a heap in the dust, his skull crushed with one vicious blow.

The razor slipped and a line of blood slowly appeared on Baruch's cheek. 'Damn.'

It brought him back to the present. He wanted to hear what Jethro and Eveline could tell him, however painful. He went back into the main room and opened the other doors carefully and quietly. His pa was asleep, wheezing. Baruch crept in. His pa's face was bloated, blotchy, bruised and all but unrecognisable. There was a huge swelling over his right eye. Baruch was torn between wanting to hold his pa and make him better, but aware that he shouldn't disturb him, letting nature take its course. He prayed silently that he would recover. In another room his ma was lying in bed. He could see the colourful bruises on her cheek and round her eyes. Quietly he went in and kissed her forehead very softly. She stirred but didn't wake. He crept out and closed the door, praying to God to speed their recovery.

Eveline was at the stove cooking up some bacon. Jethro came in with a basketful of eggs. Baruch sat down at the table. Jethro put the basket on the side and sat down with him. He spoke directly.

'What would you say if I told you Ferdy wasn't your brother, but he was your cousin?'

'Cousin? So whose child was he?'

Jethro looked over at Eveline. She pursed her lips and nodded. Jethro sighed. 'Ferdy was Erik's boy.'

'Erik!'

Jethro held up his hand. 'I know, boy, that'll be a helluva shock for you, but it's the truth.'

'But why. . . .'

'Yes, why?' Jethro said, tilting his head this way and that. 'Look, we don't know exactly what was going on, but we know that Erik sent Ferdy to your parents and they agreed to bring him up until Erik

BARUCH ELIAS

could come and get him back.'

'Get him back? Where did Erik go that he couldn't take Ferdy with him? What about Erik's wife, didn't she want him?'

'They were living in Maple Cross. We heard that Erik's wife, Leila, had turned him in just after Ferdy was born. She wanted a proper life with a proper hard-working, decent husband. She wanted Erik to go straight with his new family responsibilities, but he wouldn't, he was a born robber, a cattle rustler. She told the marshal. Erik found out and struck her. He might not have meant to hit her so hard but she died on the spot. At the time he was running a cattle-rustling gang with an accomplice named Snag Hampton. They were caught and committed to the prison in Maple Cross, but because Erik had killed Leila he was tried for that too.'

Eveline looked over her shoulder. 'How do you like your bacon, son? And Jethro, you got to tell him.'

'Just let the fat crisp up, thanks, Eveline.'

Jethro continued. 'He struck Leila down with one blow and she never recovered. He tried to say at his trial he didn't mean to kill her, but the judge said different. Gave him a ten-year stretch in the state penitentiary up near Salt Lake City. Then while he was in there he killed another prisoner, and so the sentence went on a lot longer. Anyway, when he was sent down in '59, I think it was, just before the war, there was no one to look after little Ferdy, so he came to his aunt and uncle – that's your ma and pa.

You two grew up like brothers. You were eight, Ferdy was just a baby and you didn't know he wasn't your real brother. That's all we know. I don't think anybody in Vendigo knew the baby wasn't your parents' own child, excepting us, because we were always so close.'

Baruch was looking glum. 'I guess that explains why we were always competing. I used to be jealous that he got all the attention. Now I guess they were just anxious to look after him proper. Did Erik know that Ferdy was killed by a stallion?'

Jethro shook his head. 'That wasn't any old stallion. It was Erik's horse.'

'Erik's horse! Gee, that explains why Ferdy tried to ride it that day, little fool. We were arguing about who was the better horseman, he was desperate to prove he could ride that bronco.'

Eveline spoke up. 'When Erik sent the horse with Ferdy there was a note saying to give the stallion to Ferdy for his eleventh birthday.'

'And that day was his birthday. Now I understand. Pa must have told him and he came running out to claim his stallion. I held him back. He broke free and crashed into the horse.'

Jethro said, 'Nobody dared tell Erik that Ferdy was dead.'

'So he didn't know? Is that why Erik came back to Vendigo now? Must have just got out of prison and come to see his son.'

'That's possible. Quite likely. It seems Erik turned up in the afternoon with some other riders. They went to see the sheriff and then across to your folks' shebang. There was arguing and shouting. Erik came out in a blind rage. He rode up Main Street firing his guns into the air. I was in the Silver Cactus saloon and ran out like other folk. Erik turned at the end of Main Street, reloaded and rode back again, swearing and cussing and saying he'd be back. The last shot he fired he aimed through the window of your parents' store.'

'Then he came back and burnt them out?'

'Yes, later that day, the four of them rode back into town. Erik went in and threw your ma out. She fell down the steps badly bruised. He beat up your pa and left him to die. They torched the place, stood their ground for a moment, guns drawn to stop anyone getting close. When the fire had taken hold they rode off.'

'And Sheriff Hempson?'

'Just stood in his office, watching. Anyway, we got your pa out and tried to douse the fire, but it couldn't be done. I expect Jake told you the rest.'

Baruch was thinking. 'So, Erik went to the sheriff's office first before he went to the store? Why did he do that? Mighty suspicious that the sheriff then did nothing. That can't be a coincidence. I'm going to ride into town and see what else I can find out. Who owns the Silver Cactus? Maybe I'll start there.'

Jethro shrugged. 'The barkeep's a man named Bosh – don't know his real name – but the saloon is owned by the sheriff, so be careful if you ask questions: Hempson will get to hear about it.'

'That might just be right handy,' Baruch said with a deliberate nod of his head.

He finished up his bacon, eggs and coffee and galloped into town. He rode straight up to the Silver Cactus saloon.

7

The streets of Vendigo were bustling with trade. Carts, buggies, carriages and wagons were moving up and down bringing things in from the surrounding hinterland: animals, local produce, consumer goods from travelling salesmen. A similar assortment of vehicles was taking goods back out: farm equipment, household goods and foodstuffs. People were going in and out of the many shops, stores and offices. There was even the sound of a piano coming from the bar of the Silver Cactus. Vendigo Bluff was growing prosperous on the rumour of silver deposits in the nearby hills, but as yet nobody had struck a vein of anything.

On the back of the speculation it was obvious that new trades and professions were springing up along Main Street. A newly built assay office, a mining claims office, more lawyers of course, and another bank was under construction. It would have been a boom time for the Elias hardware store. The fire had come at the worst possible moment, unless . . .

unless you were a competitor about to set up and cash in on a boom.

Baruch dismounted outside the Silver Cactus to the tune of *My Pretty Little Maid*, which rang out from the ivories. When Baruch entered the premises, he saw the keys were being tickled by a Negro with a red silk waistcoat and a black top hat. The pianist looked up, smiled at Baruch with teeth that shone a brilliant white.

'Beer please, Bosh,' Baruch said to the barman as he walked past the piano. 'And one for the pianist.'

'He only drinks whiskey,' the barman replied. 'And who told you my name, stranger?'

'Give him a whiskey then. And I ain't no stranger, Bosh. Jethro told me your name, Jethro Gilling. My name's Baruch Elias. I was brought up here. You know my folks, of course.'

The barman stopped mid-pull and his mouth dropped open. 'Baruch Elias? My, you've grown a bit, boy. Haven't seen you for, what six, seven years mebbe. That's a terrible thing, the fire. Your folks didn't deserve that.'

'Four years,' Baruch corrected. 'I left four years ago. What do you know about the fire?'

'Same as anyone. They say it was your pa's brother came into town, had a quarrel, got all fired up, then he went wild and started shooting. Came back later and done them things to your folks and set the place on fire.'

'Why didn't the sheriff stop them?'

The barman finished pulling the beer and pushed

the glass towards Baruch. 'Who says he didn't?'

'Come on, Bosh, I know he didn't, and so do you.'

'Nothing anybody could do. They just stood there with their guns drawn ready to shoot down anyone who tried to put out the fire. Then they rode off and folk did what they could. Pulled your pa out and helped your ma. You staying with the Gillings?'

'Yeah.' Baruch paused to take a long swig of beer. He wiped his mouth on his sleeve. 'Can I ask you something, Bosh? What d'you know about Sheriff Hempson and his cattle-rustling days?'

Bosh shook his head. 'Don't know nuthin' 'bout that. Don't sound right to me.'

Baruch gave the barman a long hard stare eye to eye, until the barman looked away. Baruch strolled over to the pianist with the whiskey. 'There you go, fella.'

He put the glass on top of the piano.

The Negro nodded his head sideways in grateful recognition and started playing a version of the very popular *Nobody Knows the Trouble I've Had*. It struck a chord with Baruch and he wondered if the tune was a deliberate selection. He leant down to the pianist's ear.

'Do you know anything about Hempson and cattle rustling?'

The pianist's eyes widened with a look of horror. He turned away from Baruch abruptly and looked across at the barman, then down at the keyboard. Such a deliberate action told Baruch he was on the right lines. People were afraid of Hempson and with

a bit of luck his questions would find their way back
to the sheriff. But he had to be careful. It was all very
well to rake up a bit of dirt to get people excited
without it turning into a dust storm that got out of
hand.

On reflection he wished he hadn't told Bosh he
was staying with the Gillings, just in case anyone
decided to burn them out too. There was something
going on, but he couldn't act alone against the
sheriff of a town the size of Vendigo without there
being consequences. Perhaps he should lie low for a
while.

Just then a man wearing a star pushed in through
the batwings and stood arms akimbo looking round
the room. It was one of the deputies Baruch had
seen in the sheriff's office. His gun was drawn, but
pointing at the floor. He signalled to Baruch.

'You, sonny. Come with me.'

The sudden intervention took Baruch by surprise.
Blazes, he thought; news travels even faster than he
would have expected.

'Me? What d'you want with me?'

'The sheriff needs your help.'

This was a most unlikely story. The card players at
the back of the room looked up momentarily, saw
the deputy, and carried on with their game.

Baruch had no option. He left the saloon with the
deputy and they walked in silence along the boardwalk to the sheriff's office. Baruch noticed people
gave him a look as they walked past – not unfriendly,
just curious. Perhaps the deputies had a reputation

for taking people in. He wasn't worried; he'd soon find out what all this was about, and nothing was likely to happen in broad daylight.

The deputy opened the door and stood back. Baruch went in. Hempson was sitting behind his desk smoking a cigar, as usual. The other deputy was standing by the table with the map still spread out. Baruch hesitated. The sheriff spoke first.

'Now, son, we've been doing some research. Thought we ought to help you, in case you get the wrong idea about us. That there map shows all the main cattle trails in the area and all the owners of the various ranches. Go and have a look at it. Miller will show you what we mean. That's Miller, my deputy by the map, and the other one's Voss, who came to get you. Show him, Miller.'

Baruch went over to the table. Miller, a tall, broad-shouldered man, with a tough line to his mouth and a mean look in his eye, jabbed a finger on the map.

'Vendigo is here. Out that way's Mercer's Hole. You know it? Well, we think the man you want might be out that way.'

Baruch was amazed. He didn't know what to think. Were they actually trying to help him after all? Had he misjudged them so badly? And now here they were telling him something he already knew to be true. It didn't make sense.

'I owe you an apology, Sheriff.'

'What for?'

'Suggesting you were looking at this map for . . . for something else.'

'Did you?' Hempson queried. 'It's a good job you didn't mean anything by it. You're young, maybe a bit hotheaded, and you've had a nasty shock with your folks being beat up and the shebang burnt down. I can spare Voss for a day or two if you want to go out to Mercer's Hole and search around. Why don't you go an' get your horse and get going before dark? Miller will go out to the Gillings and tell them where you've gone. The sooner you get on the trail the better, what do you say?'

Baruch swallowed hard. If anything ever sounded like a trap, this was surely it.

'It sounds a good plan. But I heard there were four horsemen doing the shooting. I can't take on four men, even with one of your deputies. Do you know who those horsemen were?'

Hempson shook his head. 'I don't think they were anything to do with it. Just the one man, Erik Elias.'

Baruch knew that was a lie. He decided on a direct approach. 'Why did he come and see you first, before he went to see his brother?'

'He came in here, as bold as you and . . . and er . . . yes, that was it, he asked if I knew who he was.'

'And did you?'

'Never seen him before.' The sheriff was looking down at his boots, a sure indication he was lying.

But Baruch still didn't know why. 'Ever heard of the Benson brothers?'

Hempson opened the drawer and rifled through some papers. He pulled out the dodger, the same one that was in Morgan's slicker. 'You mean these two?'

91

'Yes. That's them. Have you seen them?'

'No, I ain't, but I'd like to catch 'em and lock 'em up. The reward money's good.'

Now Baruch knew he was going to get nothing but lies from the sheriff. All the evidence pointed to Erik with Morgan and the Benson brothers being the four horsemen. The only reason for the sheriff to lie was because he was also involved, but how? Should he be pressed any further?

'Someone told me it was the Bensons that rode in with Erik. Could that be true?'

There was a sudden change of atmosphere. Miller stepped forward, his eyes narrowed aggressively. 'You're asking too many questions.' He struck Baruch across the cheek with the back of his hand. 'The sheriff offered to help you out. Take his advice and go with Voss to Mercer's Hole.'

It was a sharp reminder that he was in a dangerous situation and had to play his cards carefully. One wrong step and everything could turn sour.

'I didn't mean no offence,' Baruch said quickly to correct any wrong impression. 'If Voss is ready, then let's go.'

Miller stepped forward. 'I'll take him, Hempson. I know what to do.'

The sheriff looked to Miller and nodded. 'Do what you have to.'

It was late afternoon by the time Baruch rode out of town with Miller. He was hoping they would be going along Main Street so he could make a point of people seeing him, to let them know he was riding out with Miller, just in case anything bad happened to him. But Miller's horse was tied at the back of the sheriff's office and he was told to meet Miller at the back. They rode off together riding parallel with Main Street almost completely unseen. It didn't bode well.

Out of Vendigo, instead of taking the main road to Mercer's Hole, they rode across rough country in the right direction but off the track. Miller didn't speak to Baruch as they picked their way through cactus, yucca, sagebrush and scrub, occasionally following the sandy course of a dried stream. It was hard going and Baruch wondered why they weren't on the main track. When they had ridden for about an hour, he decided to ask the question.

'Is this the right track, Miller? I thought the trade road would be quicker.'

'Short cut, trust me.'

It was no reassurance at all. There was no short cut to Mercer's Hole. At least none that would make much difference to the travel time and in the distance there appeared to be a significant ridge blocking the route.

'Is there a way across that ridge?' Baruch asked.

'I don't think so.'

'Then. . . .'

'Look, kid, I've got to tell you, you've got yourself into something that you should've let go. Stay calm and don't draw on me, I ain't goin' to do you no harm.'

Baruch was beginning to wonder what was going

on. 'So why are we riding this way? I guess we never were going to Mercer's Hole.'

'No, we never were. You know who's at Mercer's Hole?'

Baruch wondered if he was going to get another lie. 'Who?'

'Erik Elias. You've nearly got yourself killed by shooting questions in Vendigo 'bout Hempson and cattle rustling. Now I'm going to come clean with you, son. I'm not really a deputy here in Vendigo. I'm a US marshal and I've been gathering evidence about cattle rustling and robberies for the last twelve months. Let's stop here a while. Unsaddle the horses and let them graze.'

Baruch climbed down, loosened the cinch and removed the saddle. He wanted to impress the marshal. 'Is Hempson his real name?'

Miller placed his saddle on the ground, sat down with his back against it and stretched his legs. 'Why do you ask that?'

'I heard that Erik Elias was working his cattle-rustling outfit with a man named Hampton, and it just seemed to me Hampton and Hempson were very similar names, so if Hampton was wanting to change his name and start a new life then Hempson might be his choice. So Snag Hampton became Greg Hempson, settled in Vendigo Bluff, and used his money to buy influence and get elected as sheriff.'

'Tell you somethin', boy, you've got a career in law enforcement with a brain that sharp, ever thought of it? Anyway, go on, what else do you think?'

'I know the sheriff was lying to me. I think Erik went to see Hempson because Hempson is his old partner in the cattle-rustling business. He went to tell him what he was going to do and not to get in his way.'

'Well you're nearly right with that, but it actually went a bit deeper. Erik threatened that if he interfered he'd expose him as a cattle thief and finish his career.'

'Blackmail.'

'Kinda,' Miller confirmed.

'Would it help if I could find out more about Erik Elias for you? After all, he is my uncle, and I need to get even with him for what he's done to my folks. I know exactly where he's hiding . . . at least I think I do.'

Miller leant back against his saddle to think for a moment. He took out a packet of tobacco and rolled himself a smoke. It was obvious while he was doing this he didn't want to be interrupted. Baruch looked on. When Miller had finished rolling, and had put a match to his cigarette he looked at Baruch with appraising eyes.

'You are one lucky son-of-a-gun,' Miller said, leaning his head back and blowing out a long stream of smoke into the sky. 'If Voss had brought you out here, you'd be asking Saint Peter to open the gates and let you in. I had a hunch you were a good kid and I didn't want to see you killed for no reason.'

Baruch felt a little offended. 'I can take care of myself,' he said, getting to his feet. He stood a few yards away from Miller and turned sideways. 'I'll show you.' He set his feet slightly apart and stood relaxed with his right hand slightly below his holster. Then in a sudden upward movement he pulled his gun and was ready to shoot.

'Yeah. Reckon you might survive. That's mighty fast for a farmhand. Where did you learn to draw like that?'

'Taught myself. Watched men at the fair when it came to town. Asked some to show me how to draw, but what I noticed was that they always lost time by going down then up again. I thought if I could just go straight up it would be quicker. So I practised leaning a little to the right to get my hand below the gun, and found it was quite easy to pull and be ready.'

'But why?' Miller insisted.

Baruch shrugged. 'Dunno. I practise with the rifle too. I have to keep an eye out for coyote and that sort of thing on the ranch.'

'Well, like I said, you've got a change of career, if you want it.'

Baruch shook his head. 'No, thanks. I've got a girl. I want to marry her and settle down to a good family life. Your job's too dangerous for a married man. Say, are you married?'

'No, son. You're right. Ain't no job for a man with a wife and kids.'

'Well, what are you going to do with me now?' Baruch asked. 'I guess you ain't goin' to shoot me in the back, like Voss might have done. So what happens now?'

'Don't you worry about me; I've got everything sorted. You just have to keep out of the way. Get back to the Gillings under cover of darkness tonight and stay hidden there until you hear that the rustlers have been arrested. I've just about got all the evidence I need to take them in. Once they're out of the way you'll be safe to leave, but don't go into Vendigo. I don't know how Voss is going to react when he finds out who I am.'

'And what about Erik? Does he go free?'

'Let me get his partner into jail at Maple Cross. Then I'll go after Erik Elias and they can both face justice together. You said you know where Erik is hiding.'

Baruch took up a stick and drew in the sand. 'Yes, a cave about half an hour north of Mercer's Hole, east across the open ground to the river. There's a clump of cottonwood stands up above the willow. There's a small enclosure for horses and a hole in the rockface. It's not easy to find.'

'I'll find it. Now you get yourself back on your horse. Skirt well to the south and hide out with the Gillings. That way I can keep you safe, so long as I know where you are.'

Baruch saddled up and bent down to shake Miller's hand, knowing that further words were unnecessary, and left the marshal to finish his cigarette.

Taking care to keep away from the beaten track, Baruch circled south of Vendigo until he could turn to the west and head for the Gillings ranch. It was getting dark. The dog would bark in the yard to alert the Gillings and Jethro would come out with his shotgun. Baruch hoped Jethro wouldn't fire off a round before realizing who was riding into the yard. At least there was a fair chance the dog would recognise him.

Picking his way across the rough ground by the light of the moon, Baruch eventually neared the ranch. A kerosene lamp was burning in the yard, and that was a good sign. As Baruch approached he could see Jethro standing on the veranda holding up the lamp, but there was a rider dismounting whom Baruch couldn't see clearly enough. Was it Voss, just coming out with the message from the sheriff that Baruch wouldn't be back tonight? Jethro invited the rider in and, taking the lamp with him, the yard fell into darkness. If it was Voss, he dared not approach any closer until the rider had left.

He pulled up and slipped down quietly off the horse. He waited and waited, but the rider didn't come out. What was going on? What was Voss doing? Were the Gillings in danger?

It was getting very cold as the temperature dropped to an uncomfortable degree. Baruch couldn't stay out any longer; he'd have to go down and see. He hobbled Whitey, apologizing for having to shackle him, and started to walk down into the yard. A moment later the dog started barking. The ranch house door opened and a figure came out. A blast of shotgun pellets flew into the air with an ear-splitting explosion.

'Come on out! Get out where I can see you!'

Then there was another figure standing behind, also carrying a gun.

8

Of course, it couldn't be Voss, why hadn't he realized that? Voss must have been out much earlier in the day to tell the Gillings that he wouldn't be back. He called out: 'Jethro! It's me, Baruch. Don't shoot! I've just got to get the horse and come down.'

The two men waited on the veranda while Baruch rode down into the yard.

'You're lucky Pa didn't shoot you,' Jake said.

Baruch laughed. 'That's the second time today I've been lucky on that account. Good to see you, Jake. If I'd been thinking straight I'd have realized it was you, only I thought it might be Voss.'

'Don't mention that name again,' Jethro rebuked. 'I ain't got time for that lazy twister. He's a bad lot, you stay clear of him.'

'Yes,' Baruch agreed. 'He was supposed to shoot me out in the desert. . . .'

'How did you get away?' Jake asked.

'It's a long story. I'd like to come in and have a bite to eat. . . .'

'Of course,' said Jethro. 'Jake, what are we thinking about? Eveline'll be pleased to see you. Come on in.'

They went in and closed the door. It wasn't long before Baruch was sitting down to a hot stew with the Gillings. During the meal he told them everything that he now knew about Erik, the sheriff and Voss, but he didn't give away anything about Miller, thinking that the fewer the people who knew he was really a marshal, the better. When he asked after his parents he was glad to hear that his ma was mending well and would be able to talk to him the next day. The news about his pa was not so good; he was unexpectedly still out of consciousness and the doc's prognostication wasn't rosy.

By the time the meal was finished and they had exhausted all their conversation, everyone retired to bed. Baruch was ready to slip away into one of the outbuildings if the need should arise, but he didn't think anyone would come looking for him in the dead of night – after all, only Miller knew he was there.

The next day dawned with a clear blue sky, deep blue at first as the sun pulled itself out of the night, and then paling over the horizon and intensifying into the heavens. In the same way, Baruch's hatred for Erik Elias had started out as a vague confusion that gradually turned into an intense desire for revenge and now hatred for what he had done.

After breakfast with his ma, Hedda, sitting in the

rocking chair on the veranda, it was time to find out what she could tell him about Erik Elias and why he'd burnt them out.

He winced at the sight of her bruised face. 'How are you feeling, Ma?'

Hedda put her hand out and touched her son lightly on the arm. 'Mending. I'm mending. It's your pa I'm worried about. Erik beat Nils to within an inch.'

'Ma, I don't want to upset you, but I've got to know what happened the other day and why Erik came back and burnt down the store.'

'Erik's a bad lot, always has been.'

'He has to be brought to justice.'

Hedda shook her head. 'That ain't goin' to be easy; he's wild and dangerous.'

Baruch played it down. 'I've got help, and I know where he's hiding.'

'Listen, son, you've always blamed yourself over Ferdy, but it weren't nothin' you should feel guilty about. We were devastated when you went away to the Sigurrsons.'

'I had to go, Ma.'

'I know. Your pa and I, we both knew. I wanted to come after you, but your father said no, I was to let you go. You had to come to terms and grow up in your own way. Look at you, you're a fine young man.'

'I couldn't live with what I'd done. Ferdy died because of me. Thank God I had the Sigurrsons to turn to, or I might have gone to the bad side myself.'

Hedda turned to Baruch and smiled. 'The

Sigurrsons are good people. As you know we came across the Atlantic together on the same ship. Arnie's wife, Mira, died in childbirth. It was so sad. Arnie lost both his wife and his unborn son. We remained firm friends with him and his little daughter, Ingrid. How is she?'

'She isn't a little girl any more.'

Hedda didn't say anything. She looked sideways at Baruch, and when his cheeks coloured slightly she didn't need to ask any more questions.

Baruch could see his ma was thinking, wrestling with an idea or something. He knew not to interrupt; she had something important to tell him and he had to wait for her to say it.

'Ferdy wasn't your brother,' she said slowly, and then much quicker, 'I know you always thought he was, an' the two of you grew up together as if you were. An' you thought he was our favourite. But it weren't like that.'

Baruch had already heard this from Eveline and hadn't quite taken it in. He couldn't quite grasp the meaning of something that seemed so wrong, so incredibly wrong. Ferdy was his brother and Baruch had caused his death. He turned to his ma. On his tongue were a million questions that he couldn't quite articulate. His ma continued.

'Ferdy was Erik's son.'

'Yes, I heard that from Eveline, but I didn't want to believe it.'

'Now listen to me. I told you Erik was a bad lot. As soon as we landed in New York he was in trouble

103

with the authorities, accused of robbing someone. I don't know whether he did or not, but because of that he never felt welcome in this country. Anyhow, we all moved out west and bought land to farm. Things went well for a while, then Erik started to neglect his land up near Maple Cross and started doing bad things, robbing and stealing and who knows what? He was never satisfied with raising stock and growing food, said it was a waste of life. He was always leaving his wife, Leila to fend for herself.'

'Just like that? With no protection?'

'He didn't really care. I think he was off having fun with loose women, you know, chorus girls and the like, those that tag along behind miners and gamblers. They'll always be women ready to take dollars off men in return for, for. . . . Well, anyways, things went from bad to worse. Erik got into cattle rustling with a man named Hampton. Leila had just given birth. He had a helluva argument with her and struck her across the face.'

'Sonofabitch! What sort of a man does that?' Baruch wondered.

'A coward,' his ma replied. 'Erik's a bully and a coward.'

'And Leila died from the blow.'

Hedda let out a big sigh. 'Leila was a lovely girl. When we were all on the boat together we had some wonderful evenings. The world was going to be a whole new place, full of opportunities. The Sigurrsons had travelled already from Iceland to get a boat to America. We got on well with them straight away. It was a tough voyage but fun. Then when Mira died it kinda brought home to us the harsh reality of what we might be coming to. We'd had too many bad winters in Sweden and life was hard. We wanted to get away from that. Along came this opportunity to emigrate to America. They wanted farmers, miners, construction workers ... anybody who wanted a new life and had the skills to make a living. So your pa and his brother Erik decided to make a break and come to America – all of us, including you. Meeting the three Sigurrsons on board, we made a good party together. You and Ingrid played a lot of chasing games on deck.'

'You don't regret it, do you?'

'Not at all. We've had a good life here until now. Leila heard about Erik's cattle rustling and tipped off the marshal. She just wanted a good husband who would look after her and Ferdy, and she hated him being away. When she told Erik she'd tipped off the marshal, he went wild. That single blow that Erik gave her killed her instantly. The coward left the ranch and rode off somewhere – Mercer's Hole, I think – and got blind drunk. It was only when some friends took him back to his ranch that the horror of what had happened was discovered. Poor little Ferdy was found in his crib. Erik was arrested for cattle rustling. Then he was given ten years for murder, rustling and robbery. We took Ferdy in and brought him up as our own son. You were eight, you didn't really understand and so you thought he was your brother. We told you he was your brother.'

Baruch held up his hand to stop the flow of information. 'Ma, this is a lot to take in all in one go.'

'It's the only way you'll understand why Erik burnt us out. Being in prison for so long did him no good. He was even worse in prison. He killed men in fights and his sentence got longer and longer.'

'But he's out now.'

'Yes, and there was only one thing on his mind: to get his son back. He wanted to see Ferdy. It was why he came to Vendigo.'

'And you had to tell him Ferdy was dead.'

'We'd kept it from him all these years. When he pitched up the other day in the store we couldn't believe it. Didn't even recognize him at first. He demanded to see Ferdy. We had to tell him what happened, about the accident.'

'It wasn't an accident,' Baruch said. 'It was my fault, I was responsible for what happened.'

'No, son. Never. Tell me what you think happened.'

Baruch shrugged. He didn't want to relive the happenings of that afternoon. 'I should never have let him get near that stallion. I tried to stop him, I knew it would end badly.'

'There's no way you could have stopped him. It was his birthday. The stallion was to be his on his eleventh birthday.'

'I didn't know that. All I saw was Ferdy come running out and heading straight for the corral. I tried to stop him. I pulled him back to stop him. If I had been holding him, he wouldn't have gone crashing into the stallion and been kicked in the head.'

Hedda put her hand on Baruch's arm and gently stroked him. 'It was an accident, son, you weren't to blame.'

'So . . . Erik didn't know Ferdy was dead.'

'Erik came straight from prison up north, rode down here to Vendigo with hardly any breaks. We had to tell him that Ferdy had died in an accident. Unfortunately I said you were trying to protect Ferdy and Erik immediately went berserk and accused you of killing his son. He came back later all boozed up and demanded to know where you were. He made it obvious that as you had taken away Ferdy, he was going to take you away from us.'

'To kill me? Jake didn't mention that!'

'He started beating your pa, demanding to know where you'd gone. Your pa wouldn't say, so Erik kept on hitting him until I couldn't stand it any longer. I didn't want to say exactly where you'd gone, so I told him you were working a ranch at Mercer's Hole. That's when he doused the place in fuel, set fire to it and rode off, shooting everywhere with his three friends, shouting that he was going to find you and kill you. That's why Jake came to warn you.'

Baruch sighed. 'That explains a lot of things. I know where Erik is hiding out, near Mercer's Hole, but I didn't know he was looking for me.' He leapt up out of the chair. 'By God, they were going off to Vimy Point. If they find the Sigurrson ranch and ask questions, Ingrid and Arnie are in danger. Listen,

Ma, I must go and warn them.'

'Don't go alone, son. Jake will go with you.'

Baruch shook his head. 'No, Jake must go and see Deputy Miller. I must speak to Jake.'

He bent down, kissed his ma on the cheek. 'I'm so glad you're mending, and I hope the same goes for Pa.'

He went inside to grab Jake, and moments later he was saddling up his horse. It would be a two-day ride. Eveline came out with a hastily wrapped packet of food, followed closely by Jethro and Jake.

'This will keep the wolf from the door,' Eveline said.

'Take care, Baruch,' was Jethro's parting shot.

Jake just nodded in recognition of what he was going to do. He, too, would be riding out soon, but he would be heading into Vendigo while Baruch would be making all haste to Vimy Point and the Sigurrson ranch.

Glad that he'd got his horse and equipment back from the Benson brothers, Baruch had all his things that would enable him to stay out the night and sleep under the stars. It would be too dangerous to stay in hotels just in case he was being followed, or if the Bensons were making enquiries. After all, hotels were the most likely place to come across a traveller.

Making the most of daylight, Baruch pressed on and was able to get a fair few miles between himself and Vendigo before he stopped to give the horse a rest and brew himself a cup of coffee. While he was collecting brushwood for the fire he was thinking about Ingrid constantly, and what he would do to anyone who tried to harm her or Arnie. He knew Arnie could take care of himself, but the Benson brothers were a pair of clever crooks, and if Erik wanted them to find Baruch they would eventually come across the Sigurrson ranch, and they would stop at nothing to get the information they wanted.

In order to keep away from the main routes, Baruch had to take a wide circle to the south. He was tempted to stake out the cave where he knew the Bensons were hiding out and ascertain if the other man really was Erik Elias. But if he did and discovered that it was Erik, what then? He could hardly walk in and say, 'Hello, I'm Baruch, who you're trying to kill.' On the other hand, maybe if Baruch could actually get to talk to Erik and explain what happened, now that he had a better understanding of it, Erik might see sense. Blood should be thicker than water. But look what Erik had done to his brother. . . .

Maybe he shouldn't have left Vendigo. Perhaps he should have talked this over with Miller before acting so precipitously. But how? How would he get to Miller without Hempson knowing, or without blowing Miller's cover? No, he would have to rely on the original plan and hope that Jake could get the message to Marshal Miller.

He kicked out the fire and saddled up, secured the cinch and, grabbing the reins, swung up.

No sooner had he turned Whitey than two bullets kicked up dust right under the horse. In one swift movement, Baruch slid off the saddle and pulled the horse back quickly to a deep arroyo. He took cover and pulled the Winchester out of the scabbard, then lay down on the bank such that he could just look over the edge to try and spot what was going on. Had someone taken a shot at him, or was he just in the way of some other incident? In his state of heightened tension he quickly assumed that the shots were meant for him or his horse. But who had fired them? He peeled his eyes and scanned the area as far as he could see.

A bird swooped between two cacti. The sudden movement caught his eye but there was nothing else to see. Then he spotted something in a clump of scrubby vegetation. A couple of low bushes and a single tall spike of succulent, barely enough to hide a dog, let alone a man. But he was sure there was someone hiding there.

9

At least he had pulled his horse to safety in the deep, dry arroyo. He couldn't stand cowards who shot horses to get at the rider. It would have been quite easy for Baruch to put a couple of shots into the brush, aiming below the tall spike of the succulent and have a fair chance of winging whoever it was in there. He was just deciding what to do when a shout rang out.

'Baruch, Baruch Elias!'

It was a strange dismembered voice that called out from the brushwood.

The voice called again. 'Stand still, you son of a gun! And don't shoot. I ain't going to harm you.'

Baruch scanned for the body that belonged to the voice. He waited and watched. Slowly, a figure crawled out from under the brushwood. The speed with which he emerged, or rather the slowness, suggested he wasn't a young man. Baruch couldn't identify him.

'It's me, Mart. You remember? The Silver Cactus.'

111

Baruch pulled his horse back out of the arroyo and put the Winchester back in the scabbard. Mart came across to him, a rifle held loosely in his hand. His wrinkled face was almost in a smile, or perhaps he was just squinting in the sun.

'Mart, what the hell? You could have shot the horse.'

'Could've,' Mart admitted. 'And I could've shot you up the other day.'

'What d'you mean?'

Mart chuckled. 'Outside the Silver Cactus, when you were standing there watching that fight.'

'You put that on for me?'

'No. That just happened at the same time.'

'So why?'

'You introduced yourself to me as Barclay instead of Baruch. Who the hell is Barclay? I knew you were Baruch Elias and so did Tad. We've known you since you were no bigger that a prairie dog. I figured you were trying to lie low because of your folk's place being burnt down. And then all the questions you were asking . . . I wanted to warn you. You ducked off after I shot at you outside the saloon, and it's taken me all this time to track you down on your own and stop you, so I can tell you what I know.'

'It was a pretty extreme way of stopping me.'

Mart smiled. 'It did the trick. I didn't want to see you get killed asking questions about the wrong people, dangerous people.'

Baruch laughed – he couldn't help himself. 'So

what is it you know? What is it that you want to warn
me about?'

'The questions you were asking about the horsemen who were riding with Erik Elias, well they were
the Benson brothers and Morgan Creech.'

'How did you know that?'

Mart tapped the side of his nose. 'You know, son,
I was a deputy here a while back, before Hempson
came along. You don't remember me, no reason why
you should. I remember 'bout that stallion and what
it done to Ferdy and your parents, and you for that
matter. Anyways, when Hempson was elected the
new sheriff, I turned in my badge. And another
thing: Hempson and cattle rustling. I said I didn't
know anything about that, but I do. One thing I
know is that if you go asking questions about that
you'll get yourself killed.'

Baruch reflected on that for a moment. It had
indeed nearly got him killed, if it hadn't been for the
intervention by Miller.

'So I appreciate everything you've said, Mart, but
I gotta tell you I knew all that already.'

'You did?'

'Yep.'

Mart looked quite crestfallen. 'But there's one
thing you don't know. One of the deputies is not
who he says he is.'

Baruch knew Mart was going to tell him about
Miller, but decided to humour the old-timer.

'Oh? Which one?'

'Voss.'

Baruch did a double-take. 'Voss? Voss?!'

'Ah, you didn't know that, did you?' Mart almost jumped for joy, his grey eyes sparkled. 'See, I knew I could help you out. When you were asking about Hempson, you were asking about the wrong man.'

'Really? Hempson used to be called Hampton . . .'

'Tosh and nonsense!' Mart exclaimed, throwing his head back and laughing out loud. 'Hampton changed his name to Voss. Hampton was in the cattle rustling business with your uncle Erik Elias. Now I don't know what that's got to do with Erik burning down your folks' store, but I do know you need to be careful before you go round accusing the wrong people. . . .'

Baruch wasn't listening to Mart anymore. If this was true, Miller had lied to him about having gathered all the evidence against Hempson. Miller had even agreed that Baruch had correctly identified Hempson as Erik's old partner. Why? If Miller had lied about that, what was he up to? Now, on reflection, had Baruch sent Jake into a trap with a message for Miller? What if Miller and Voss were partners and the only honest one was actually Hempson? What a mess!

'. . . and that could land us all in trouble!' Mart asserted. 'Hey, sonny! You haven't been listening to a word I said.'

'Oh, I have,' Baruch lied. 'What do you know about Miller? Is he who he says he is?'

'No idea,' Mart said disappointingly. 'Anyway, I thought I'd better warn you before you went on poking your nose into affairs that might end badly.'

Baruch held out his hand to shake Mart's. 'By the way, Mart, how do I know you're on the level?'

'You don't.'

Baruch mounted up, took the reins in his hand and turned his horse, ready to ride off. Mart called up to him. 'By the way, Baruch, Miller told me to keep an eye on you.'

'Oh, when was that?'

'Yesterday.'

'So . . .'

Mart nodded his head. 'So, Miller is looking out for you. You can trust Miller.' Then as an after-thought, 'You can trust me too, buddy.'

Mart slapped Baruch's horse, which reared up immediately. Baruch was good enough to hold on tight, then waved his hat as a gesture of farewell. It was only after a short distance that he was left wondering whether the conversation with Mart should cause concern or relief. The more immediate problem was to skirt Mercer's Hole and get back to Ingrid and Arnie at Vimy Point.

He rode on until the sun had all but gone down before deciding to look for a suitable place to stop for the night. He knew he was too tired to ride on without stopping. He'd be up at first light, which would be better than stumbling about in the dark.

Finding a small scrape near the twisted branches of a long-dead fir and a thick tangle of juniper that had spread itself over a bit of a bank, he decided to make it his camp for the night. He unbuckled the cinch and removed the saddle and blanket, then the bridle. He hobbled Whitey to let him graze on whatever he could find. He unrolled his soogan and went off to gather some wood to boil water for coffee. Some biscuits and a slab of cold bacon that Eveline had wrapped up for him would do for an easy meal.

Both Baruch and Whitey settled down for the night. The moon came up and the stars winked at him, but within five minutes Baruch had sunk into a deep sleep.

He woke shortly after four in the morning, when the desert is at its coldest. The embers from last night's fire had lost practically all of their heat. He piled on the dry twigs that had been put to one side the night before and with a little gentle coaxing the smoke began to rise, soon superseded by little tongues of orange flame. Larger bits of woody debris went on and started to crackle. The noise caused some scurrying of little rodents curious to see what was going on. Baruch put his tin mug of water to boil and rolled himself a smoke while he waited for the fire to do its work.

Refreshed and relaxed after a smoke and some coffee, he gathered up his bedroll, saddled the horse and set off. It was the quietest time of day. The early birdsong had halted temporarily, and it was a bit too early for much other activity. The horseshoes in contact with the stony ground seemed to be inordinately loud. The desert doesn't come to life until the sun has warmed up the blood of its many little inhabitants. The moon was still visible as the sun rose above the horizon, and in a matter of moments night had turned into day with myriad insects buzzing round the cactus. It was going to be a long, hot day.

By late afternoon he had successfully skirted to the south of Mercer's Hole and had met nobody. He wondered whether he should risk going to Radford and meeting up with Bryce to put him in the picture, or avoid the place and sleep out under the stars once more. He felt he owed it to Bryce to tell him what had happened and fill him in on the Benson brothers.

Reaching the top of a small promontory and looking to the east, he could quite easily pick out the location of Radford. A couple of buildings standing proud near the little settlement were thrown into sharp relief by the raking light of the sun. It was about a two-hour ride away.

The sun had dipped further into the west when Baruch pulled up at the saloon and hitched his horse. He was soon being greeted by Bryce and Mary-Lou like a long lost friend. Chatting together over a glass of beer, Baruch gave Bryce the low-down on the whole episode of the Bensons, being robbed, finding the hideout, and then going to Vendigo Bluff with everything that followed thereafter.

'The sonsofbitches,' Bryce exclaimed on more than one occasion.

Baruch then tried to untangle the information he'd had from Miller and Mart. It didn't add up too good in places, but having laid it out before Bryce and listened to his interjections, it kind of made more sense. They both came to the conclusion that Miller could probably be trusted, although the questions about Hempson and Voss were still a puzzle.

Baruch took a swig of beer. 'I'm going to have to deal with Erik at some point. I want to shoot that no-good for what he's done to my folks. My pa is still unconscious. If he doesn't pull through, I'll skin Erik Elias.'

'You gotta be careful there, Baruch,' Bryce warned. 'If he's killed his wife and someone else in prison he isn't going to be easy to take.'

Baruch leapt to his feet and whipped out his gun with his upward technique and Bryce was impressed.

'But,' Bryce said, 'that depends on you being in a showdown with him. Cowards like him don't play like that.'

'I know,' Baruch admitted, 'I know. Anyway, I presume the Bensons haven't been here asking if anyone knew where they could find me.'

'Find you?'

'Yes, I told you they were instructed to come out looking for me. I'm pretty sure it was Erik in the cave. But they wouldn't come back here, not after Abel's encounter with us and Morgan being shot to death right here.'

'No, I ain't heard about anyone asking after you. Now what do you want to eat, my friend? I guess you're staying the night here.'

'I've been baking a beef pie today, will you have some of that?' Mary-Lou asked.

'Sure thing.'

It was gone midnight before Baruch turned in for the night, having enjoyed one of the best pies he'd ever eaten. It was certainly as good as any that Angelina made out at the ranch, and hers were first rate. So after a long day's ride and a convivial evening with Bryce and Mary-Lou, it took Baruch no time to disappear into the depths of sleep.

Being in a comfortable bed with proper sheets and a soft mattress, Baruch slept until gone eight o'clock next morning. When he woke he dressed quickly and almost ran down the stairs and across the road.

'I let you sleep on,' Bryce said as a greeting, standing behind the bar and cleaning some glasses. 'You were pretty tired last night.'

'I need to get going; I must get out to the ranch today and hope that the Bensons haven't yet managed to locate where I live. If they have, there could be trouble soon.'

'Do you want me to ride out with you?'

'Thanks, but no, I think I can handle it. Arnie wouldn't let anything happen, and the Bensons wouldn't do anything without Erik's say-so.'

'All right, if you're sure. Now, bacon and eggs?'

Half an hour later Baruch was saddled up and ready to go. Bryce stepped out onto the boardwalk in front of the saloon to wave him off.

'I'm here if you need me,' he said.

Baruch set off and soon left the main road to cut across country. He had already decided that it would be foolish to approach the ranch up the main track in broad daylight. Or was it a subconscious premonition? The Benson brothers had almost three days of searching since Baruch had overheard the conversation in the cave. Now that he knew from his ma that Erik was looking for him there wasn't a moment more to waste. Supposing they had managed to ask around and discover where the Sigurrson ranch was located, what would they do? Presumably they would tell Erik, and then what?

These idle musings helped to pass the journey time. Baruch hardly noticed the sun beginning its descent towards dusk until he realized the shadows were lengthening. Vimy Point had just come into view in the distance. It was time to circle round to the ranch.

The sun was sinking fast and the last half-mile was covered in near darkness, the only light coming from the paleness of the sky as the sun had gone down behind the distant mountains some while ago. At least now he was on familiar territory and not having to stumble through thickets of brushwood and cacti. Proceeding with extra caution on account of the situation rather than the terrain, Baruch came close to the large cultivated vegetable plot behind the ranch house. He dismounted and tied the horse. Instinct told him that something wasn't quite right.

If the Bensons had found that this was where Baruch lived, maybe they would stake out the ranch and wait for him to return. Was it possible that there

was a guard posted somewhere in the yard buildings? Surely they couldn't spare anyone. Baruch was
sure there was only the four of them in the cave and
they wouldn't use the woman for guard duty. No, if
they found out Baruch lived here they'd have come
blustering back and rushed into the place hoping to
find him. Erik and the Bensons were not going to do
anything quietly. Look what they had done in
Vendigo – they'd even warned the sheriff what they
were about to do and told him to keep out of the
way!

Maybe everything here was just that bit too quiet.
At this sort of time in the evening, he'd be sitting
down to a meal with Arnie and Ingrid. Angelina
would have cooked one of her stews or pies, or a slab
of beef, and they'd be chatting together round the
table digesting their food and drinking some beer or
coffee. For a moment Baruch dwelt wistfully on the
happy memory of them all being round the table,
him and Ingrid making eyes at each other, Angelina
trying to get Arnie to make her more than just a
cook and good friend.

It was just at that moment that Baruch suddenly
realized there wasn't a single lamp alight in the
house. When dusk fell, lanterns were always hung
outside the main door to the house, and of course
lamps and candles were lit inside. Without being
aware of this, the lack of light is what had subcon-
sciously been playing on his mind, a warning that
something was up. All his senses went into danger
mode and he ducked down automatically, ready to

creep up to the windows. But before that there was something else to be checked.

Keeping low, he skirted round the edge of the vegetable plot, the only cover being a couple rows of maize and some beans at half that height. Little pumpkins and squashes were ripening on the ground, and in any case, like most of the other things in the plot, they were never going to grow to any height anyway. Darkness was his only real cover and the moon was as bright as it had been lighting his way across the desert at night. However, the moon was a boon when he got to the track that led into the yard; this is what he had come to see, and there, thrown into stark relief, were the plethora of hoof prints. There was no doubt there had been a lot of activity in the last few days. It confirmed what he already feared. The question now was simply about who was inside the house.

He regained the shelter of the house and peered carefully through each window in turn. It was an impossible task. Outside was lighter than inside; he was likely to show up as a silhouette himself, and he couldn't determine what was in any of the rooms as it was too dark. So there was no alternative to going inside, but neither the main door nor a side door would be sensible. There was probably a barrier anyway, unless they thought Baruch would just go right on in through the front door.

There was one other way. A trapdoor at the back led down to the basement under the house where various things were stored that were better off in the

dark or out of the way of vermin. From the basement, a very small hatch and stepladder led directly
into the main room behind the pot-bellied stove. It
was the only possible quiet point of entry, provided
the hinges didn't scream.

Getting into the basement wasn't a problem.
Inside it was dark, but Baruch's eyes quickly accustomed as his pupils were already dilated from the
dark of the night. He could see the ladder up to the
trapdoor into the main room. He felt for the bolts.
The first one eased back without any noise. The
second one was stuck and wouldn't budge. While he
was puzzling what to do, he distinctly heard footsteps
move quietly across the floor above his head.
Someone was in the room. He waited. A piece of fur-
niture was being dragged across the floor. Seizing
the opportunity, Baruch grasped the bolt, and with
extra effort it slipped out of the bracket and the
hatch was free.

He eased it up a fraction and, placing his eye close
to the slit, he tried to make out the shapes in the
room. Moonlight was infiltrating the windows just
enough for him to see a chair had been moved
against the main door. It suggested someone was
securing the house for the night. Then he saw the
figure sitting on the floor. Legs hunched up underneath, head bent, arms tied behind. Rope round the
legs was catching what little light there was. Even in
the semi darkness, Baruch could tell it was Arnie.

It wasn't long before the moving figure came back
into the main room, probably having checked all the

windows and the other door. It was one of the Bensons. He crossed to the stove. Baruch instinctively withdrew a few inches, but he needed to see where Benson was going to place himself and then be ready in one swift movement to spring out of the hatch and overpower him before he could resist.

Baruch's breathing had become faster in tune with his heartbeat. He took a moment to steady his nerves, put one hand on the underside of the hatch ready to fling it back, and with the other drew his gun. The moment had come.

10

In one swift and easy movement, Baruch swung the hatch back and jumped out into the semi-darkness of the main room. His gun was ready to use as a cosh or, if necessary, to plug the intruder.

'Don't move, Benson!' he shouted, not knowing whether it was Kane or Abel, and not caring either.

'Wha-what?' was the only noise that came from his adversary.

Baruch had taken him completely by surprise. Startled, Benson jerked in the chair. Baruch saw the slow, deliberate movement of the hand creeping towards the holster.

'Only if you want to die!' he warned. 'Otherwise leave it alone.'

Getting closer, Baruch now recognised Abel Benson. He pulled back the firing pin and pressed the gun into the bridge of Benson's nose while he removed the six-gun from the holster.

'If you've got any other weapons, Benson, tell me now, because I'll have not the slightest hesitation in putting a bullet between your eyes.'

'You're making a big mistake, kid. You won't get away with this.'

'It's your mistake,' Baruch corrected. 'Now, light the lamp.'

Baruch stepped back, keeping the gun levelled. Benson got out of the chair, picked up the matches and lit the lamp. As soon as light spread across the room, Baruch saw that Arnie was slumped, head down on his chest, his mouth gagged, his face cut and bruised.

He prodded Benson savagely with the six-gun. 'Untie him.'

It took a while to remove the ropes and the gag. Arnie was in a bad way. He had been beaten with more than fists: there was a cut above his left eye and his face was swollen on one side. The minute Benson had finished, Baruch unleashed a vicious kick into his chest that sent him sprawling across the room, pitching up against the wall. It was retribution for what he had obviously done to Arnie.

Looking at the pathetic figure holding his chest, the first part of his intervention being accomplished in subduing Benson and releasing Arnie, the adrenaline subsided. He walked over to Benson. The desire to keep kicking him was overwhelming; it was the way Arnie had been treated as well as his pa in the Vendigo raid. Although he knew it was bordering on gratuitous violence, Baruch swung his boot into Benson's ribs.

'You sonofabitch. Where's Ingrid?'

Benson managed a lascivious sneer. 'Erik's enjoying her company right now.' He received another hefty kick in the ribs for the comment.

Baruch was taken aback for the moment. He hadn't thought about Ingrid being taken away, but now thinking about it, both the Bensons had probably ridden out to the ranch to find Baruch, and when they realized he wasn't there they'd beaten Arnie, tied him up and left Abel to wait for Baruch to show up, while Kane had taken Ingrid back to the hideout. Baruch was beginning to think he could have done with Bryce's offer of help.

Just then, Arnie seemed to perk up a bit. He spoke with difficulty, as his jaw didn't move too freely. 'Tie the sonofabitch up, and I'll look after him while you go and find Ingrid.'

Arnie staggered to his feet. Limping, he picked up the rope that he had been tied with and handed it to Baruch. He poked Abel with his boot. He could so easily have kicked him but he didn't.

'Unlike you, Benson, I don't go in for mindless violence. I pity people like you who seem to get great pleasure from causing pain to others. If we are to make anything of this fine country, we have to live by the rule of law and no other. Be thankful for that, because your fate will be in the hands of a judge and jury, not bullying scum like yourself who have no morals and no moral courage. Left to me, I'd be tempted to waste a bullet on you and rid this land of your kind of vermin. God damn you.'

Arnie spat onto the floor. He tied Abel's hands

127

behind his back then looked to Baruch to see what next. Baruch handed his gun to Arnie. 'Keep him covered.'

He pulled out a stickback chair and positioned it under a roof beam. He looped the rope round Abel's neck. 'Get on the chair.'

'You goin' to hang me?'

'No, just make sure you stay still. Now get up.'

Abel stood on the chair, he had no choice. Baruch threw the end of the rope over the rafter, pulled it down, threw it over a second time and tied it off round the chair leg.

'Best to keep still.' He turned to Arnie. 'If he gives any trouble, just kick the chair away.'

He took Arnie into the corner of the room where Abel couldn't hear him. 'Listen, I've got to go and find Ingrid. Did they harm her at all?'

'I don't think so.'

'If they have, by God they'll all hang for it. I know where their hideout is. . . .'

'How did you. . . ?'

'It's a long story, don't worry. I'll get help out here as soon as I can. I'll stop by in Radford. A chap called Bryce will come out to help you. He'll take Abel off your hands and look after him. Leave it all to me. Get your shotgun and keep an eye on Benson. Bryce will get out here as soon as he can.'

Baruch left the ranch house by the same way he came in, knowing all the doors and windows were secured. He bolted down the hatch and the trap door as he left. Out into the night, he retraced his steps to retrieve his horse.

Thinking he had successfully accomplished a neat trick, he wasn't on his guard and didn't notice a figure standing beside his horse.

'Nice work, son. It's me, Mart.'

Baruch jumped clean out of his skin.

'Jeez, Mart, I could've shot you. Where's your horse? What are you doing here?'

'I told you, Miller said to look out for you.'

'But how. . . ?'

'I just followed. I waited for you to turn in last night, before staying with Bryce.'

'You know Bryce?'

'I do now. He's just as concerned as I am, and feels better now he knows I'm looking out for you.'

It being so dark, Mart didn't see Baruch shaking his head. He was shaking it in disbelief, finding it hard to understand why everyone wanted to help him. Bryce, Mart, Miller. . . .

'Look, Mart, what should we do with Abel Benson? Arnie's been beaten up. I've tied Benson to a beam so he'll hang himself if he moves.'

They decided to leave things as they were with Arnie and Benson, and ride together back to Radford. Under the cover of darkness they didn't have to worry about meeting anyone on the road. The moon gave sufficient light to follow the sandy track. Alternating between a gallop and a fast trot, they kept their horses going at a good pace. By the time they reached Radford the sun was just getting up. Bryce was surprised to see them, but glad of it.

He offered them breakfast and they readily accepted. The horses needed a rest and so did they.

Baruch and Mart were just finishing their coffee when Bryce came over to them.

'So what's the situation at the ranch?' he asked.

'They beat up Arnie and they've taken Ingrid away. I guess they've taken her back to the cave. I've kinda secured one of the Bensons in the ranch and Arnie is keeping a watch on him. With Abel out of the way I think there's only Erik and Kane in the hideout. There's also a woman, but I don't know who she is.'

Bryce stroked his chin. 'What's your plan? I suppose you want to rescue Ingrid. Well, I'm happy to help.'

Mart said, 'We shouldn't do that yet. I think I ought to ride back to Vendigo and get Miller. I was supposed to be keeping an eye on you, Baruch, not getting you into a scrape.'

'Wouldn't it be safer to get Abe Benson back here?' Bryce wondered. 'If Arnie has been beaten up, he won't be feeling too good. What if Benson managed to get free?'

'He can't.'

'Never think that way,' Mart said. 'In my experience, anything can happen.'

It made Baruch pause for a moment. 'You're right. We need Abe Benson where we can see him. Maybe we could even use him as a bargaining chip. We could exchange him for Ingrid, perhaps.'

Mart stood up. 'Listen, you may think I'm an old-timer who doesn't know nothin', but I've seen a fair old chunk of life and I'm going to make a decision. You all right with that, Baruch?'

'Maybe.'

'Now,' Mart said firmly, 'are you going to do what I say?'

Baruch nodded.

'Right. Bryce, can you go and get Abe Benson, bring him back here and see that Arnie's all right?'

'Sure.'

'Baruch, you stay put here, don't go nowhere. I'm going back to Vendigo to get Miller. Does he know where the hideout is?'

Baruch nodded again. 'Yeah, I told him it was just north of Mercer's Hole. He'll find it. Maybe we meet up in Mercer's Hole day after tomorrow?'

Bryce was concerned. 'What if they go back to the ranch?'

'I don't think they'll do that,' Baruch guessed. 'I expect they'll wait until Abe has caught me and taken me back to the cave. There's something you'd better know: Erik wants to kill me.'

Bryce recoiled. 'Kill you!'

'Yeah. I killed his son.'

Mart just shook his head. He wasn't going to get into that discussion right now.

Half an hour later, Bryce and Mart had gone their separate ways. Baruch hadn't moved from Bryce's saloon. He had his feet up on a chair and was chatting with Bryce's wife, Mary-Lou, who'd made him some coffee. He was telling her about Ingrid and how he was hoping to marry her.

'You sound very much in love with this girl.'

Baruch agreed. 'I am, she's all I want in this world. I was kinda asking for her hand when Jake arrived with the news that my folks' place had been burnt down.'

'And now she's been kidnapped.'

'Not really kidnapped, just taken away. I expect Erik thinks I might be lured into a trap to go and find her.'

'And you don't want to go looking?' Mary-Lou wondered.

'I already know where she's been taken.'

'Then why are you sitting here?'

Baruch slid his feet off the chair, sat up and frowned. 'I can't go on my own; it's too dangerous. I understand that. Besides, Mart said to wait because he's gone for help.'

'I thought you were more adventurous than that from what Bryce had told me. Anyways, if it was me who'd been kidnapped, I'd want to know that Bryce was out looking for me, coming to rescue me, doing the right thing. Is Ingrid a pretty girl?'

'Sure thing!'

'Kidnapped by a man?'

'Two of them,' Baruch said, without thinking. He leapt up. 'Hey, are you saying why am I sitting here when there's two men with my girl?'

Mary-Lou just tilted her head.

'Hellfire! You're right. Bryce won't be back until quite late tonight and we're not meeting Mart until the day after tomorrow. Anything could happen.'

That was all it took, a snippet of conversation, a hint of inactivity, to get Baruch all boiled up over Ingrid. What a fool he'd been to think that everything would just wait until Miller arrived.

Like a bolt of lightning he was at the livery, saddled up and riding out. If Erik or Kane had laid a finger on Ingrid they'd regret it . . . they sure would.

Instead of heading west to Mercer's Hole, Baruch set off in a northwesterly direction to ride one side of the triangle instead of going west then north. Although the mountain range was running parallel with the road to Maple Cross from Mercer's Hole, the chances were good on finding a way through. Mindful that Whitey had just ridden through the night, Baruch made haste without tiring the horse. Having no plan in mind, he hoped something would come to him when he reached the cave. Any thoughts of danger, or waiting for Miller, were overridden by the seed of doubt that Mary-Lou had planted so firmly. Whatever else happened, he would see that Ingrid was safe and inviolable.

Day turned to dusk and that, in turn, became darker until the moon was well up and casting an eerie light across the landscape. Having found a crossing point, Baruch was now on the right side of the range and carefully looking for the enclosure. It wasn't easy to find, even though he knew he was in the right area. Luckily the quiet neighing of a horse alerted him to its proximity. He approached with caution. Recognising the lie of the land, the screen of brushwood and the willow brake near the cave entrance, he dismounted and tied his horse. From that point onward he kept as low a profile as possible. Other than the occasional stomping of hoofs there was no sign of life. Up close to the cave entrance, Baruch counted the horses. There were five. He couldn't remember how many there had been last time: was it four, three, or five even then? Erik, Kane, the woman. What about the other two? It was unlikely that they would only have enough horses for one each, and none of them were saddled up.

It was time to venture closer. Last time there had been the flickering light of a fire, which he hadn't approached, so there must be a larger cavern beyond the entrance tunnel. Maybe it was old mine workings, or just a natural fissure in the rock that had been used for the storage of goods, or maybe it had always been an outlaws' hideout. He waited until the horses stirred to cover his approach to the cave entrance. With his ears straining for the slightest indication of humans, Baruch crept closer to the tunnel. Safely inside, although that was the wrong way to think, he felt along the wall and moved very slowly, a step at a time.

There was a cracking of twigs that pulled him up short and made him catch his breath. The sounds were channelled into the tunnel and he couldn't be sure whether they were coming out of the cavern or from back at the entrance. He stood stock still, and then figured it was just the sound of a fire. The sound, maybe, but there was no smell of smoke. Perhaps the cavern was much bigger than he thought, or maybe there were several side tunnels and a draft was leading away from the entrance, taking the smoke out somewhere else.

Suddenly Baruch felt afraid. The true impact of what he was doing became very real. If anyone did come into the tunnel from outside he was trapped. What lay ahead of him was equally dangerous, mainly because he had no idea what it was. One thing was for sure and very disconcerting: there was no talking, no mouth organ.

Now that his ears were attuned to the quietly muffled sounds in the cave, he could make out the low level noise of the fire as it consumed the wood, and the occasional cracking of twigs or a sudden flare as something caught. Encouraged by the lack of human voices, he decided to keep moving forward. The light from the fire flickered ahead of him, but there must also be lamps casting a more even illumination, as it was too bright for just fire-light. Emboldened now that he could see the floor of the tunnel more clearly Baruch moved quickly and soon came to the final turn in the tunnel. But still no voices. Now he could see more of the cavern. An inch or two further and the fire came into view, and then. . . .

On the far side of the cavern, with its domed roof, Ingrid was sitting slumped against the wall, just like Arnie had been at the ranch, hands and legs tied in the same way. She was gagged with her head down on her chest. It was impossible to tell whether she was awake or asleep. Baruch stared for a moment, then felt a strong impulse to rush over and take her in his arms, tell her that everything would be all right, that he was here to rescue her, just like Mary-Lou had said.

Instinct held him back.

Going off from the central cavern were three other openings that must have led to further sleeping places and who knows what? One of them, up a couple of steps, looked barely high enough to stand upright; the smoke from the fire was finding its way into that one, which may have led to a chimney or air hole. So why was Ingrid tied up right there? He had so recently thought about being set up in a trap when Miller had taken him out into the desert. He had spoken to Mart about walking into a trap with Ingrid being held hostage as bait. But his heart had overruled his head. He had listened to Mary-Lou's admonition and acted on it. Looking with desperate pity on Ingrid's hunched figure, he made a move towards the fire.

11

For a moment he was intrigued by the smoke that rose in a drifting wispy line some fifteen feet or so to the cavern roof, before hugging a route into the little stepped tunnel. It was a careless distraction. He hadn't gone more than a few feet into the cavern, when he heard the ominous click of a firing pin being pulled back. He stopped dead and automatically lowered his hand to his holster. He peered into the recesses of the dark tunnels, his nerves tingling. When a voice spoke, he couldn't tell which direction it was coming from.

'That's far enough, Baruch. Drop the gun slowly to the ground and kick it away. Don't make any sudden movement, or it's goodbye Ingrid.'

At that moment Ingrid came to with a jerk and looked up startled, her eyes wide with fear.

Baruch dropped his gun and slowly raised his hands. He deliberately kicked the gun under a woodpile near the fire. A figure stepped out from one of the further tunnels. It was nobody he was expecting.

'Voss?'

'That's me, buddy,' he said, stepping forward. 'Miller should've let me finish you off in the desert, but he stepped in for whatever reason. Said he'd done the job, but look, here you are. I knew he hadn't killed you. Tied you up, maybe. Miller's too soft.'

Another figure appeared behind him. This one Baruch knew well.

Voss looked over his shoulder and saw it was Kane. He turned back to Baruch.

'I guess you've met Kane. Said you had an interesting chat down by the river in the canyon. He should have done for you then, too. Would have if he'd known who you were. A cat with nine lives maybe.'

Then another figure strode into the cave.

'Well, Baruch, at last. You were just a little nipper last time I saw you, long time ago. Guess you'd have been about seven or so when you met your new brother Ferdy. My boy, Ferdy. Great little kid, wasn't he? He was just a little baby when I had to give him up. And d'you know what I've been looking forward to all these years? The one thing that kept me going day to day in that stinking hole of a prison? Seeing my boy. All these years, waiting to see my boy. He'd be fifteen now and a fine lad.'

Baruch opened his palms in a gesture of submission. 'And I tried to save him, to hold him out of the way.'

BARUCH ELIAS

Erik nodded as he stepped forward towards the fire.
'That's what they told me. And if you hadn't, he wouldn't
have crashed into the horse. How d'you think I felt?
What did I feel when your ma told me that?'

He prodded the fire with his boot, dislodged a
medium sized branch of pine, smouldering at one
end. He bent down, picked it up and looked at the
end. Then, in a sudden swift movement, he swung it
viciously at Baruch's legs. The blow was sudden and
violent. It knocked Baruch to the ground, felled at
one swipe. He cried out in shock and pain before he
could stop himself.

'Yes,' said Erik, 'a bit like that.' He thumped his
chest with his fist. 'Right here. That's how I felt. I
guess you believe in the Bible?'

'I do.'

'Then you know what it says about an eye for an
eye, a tooth for a tooth and a life for a life.'

'Not the last one.'

'No,' Erik agreed, 'not that last one. But it should,
don't you think?'

Smarting from the pain in his leg, hoping it wasn't
broken, but staying down on the ground so as not to
rouse further passion, Baruch wanted to even up the
odds.

'We've got Abe hostage out at the ranch, you
know. Bryce and Arnie are there,' he said.

'Bryce Radford, you mean? Man with the same
name as the town? Yeah, we figured that,' Voss said
in a self-satisfied way. 'Leastways, you thought you
had that sorted. But Hempson was on his way out

139

there jest in case you decided to go there first.'

'Hempson? Is he in this too?'

'We're all in it. Little pipsqueak of a kid like you ain't goin' to interrupt our operation.' Voss seemed quite adamant on that point.

Now it was time for Baruch to start questioning things. If it came to a showdown, who would come to help him? Mart had assured him he could count on himself and Miller, but Voss seemed to question that. Bryce would certainly come to his aid. So here was Erik, Voss and Kane, and then Hempson out at the ranch. The sides might be about evenly matched. Then he thought on a bit further. Arnie was injured, Bryce might be jumped by Hempson thinking there was no opposition at the ranch, Mart and Miller would be a day's ride away.

Things were now looking very bleak.

Erik cut into his thoughts. 'You know, Baruch, I can see a use to you. Ingrid was useful for getting you here. You might be useful to see who else turns up. I've been wondering about Miller, since Voss told me he intervened to take you out to the desert to finish you off. Guess he's a bounty hunter or something. I don't know Bryce, but I don't suppose he'll amount to much.'

'Shall I tie him up?' Voss asked Erik.

'Let Kane do it. Sit him next to the girl, Benson, they can mime sweet nothings to each other.'

Kane secured Baruch's hands, pushed him over towards Ingrid, tied his legs and put a gag in his mouth.

The woman appeared. 'Are you ready to eat, boys?'

Baruch guessed it was Erik's fancy piece who he'd picked up since coming out of jail. She was dressed in the Mexican style with a wide colourful skirt and a bolero top, leaving her smooth, olive-brown shoulders exposed. She had thick dark hair and sultry eyes to match.

There was probably a charcoal stove down one of the tunnels, since there were no cooking pots on the fire.

'Give them a bowl of stew, Pia. Get outside when you've got your grub, Voss, and keep watch. Benson, keep an eye on these two.'

For the moment, things had calmed down.

Voss got his grub and disappeared down the tunnel towards the cave entrance. Kane stood up, eating noisily from his bowl. Erik and his woman, Pia, went back into the passageway that they had emerged from. It sounded like more than a few yards away, down some steps. Soon the sounds of eating and chatting were drifting back up into the cave.

Baruch moved closer to Ingrid. He could see her fear, but also the tenderness. He put his cheek close to hers and they felt the warmth of each other's face. He tried to reassure her with his eyes. A plan was forming in his head. Kane finished his grub and went down the tunnel, presumably to get more. Baruch heard Erik and Kane start up a conversation.

He eased himself across the floor, moving quickly

like a caterpillar by hunching his knees then sliding along. He got to the fire, looked carefully for a suitable stick, moved it with his foot and, turning round, felt for it and pulled it free. He slid his way back to Ingrid and indicated for her to use the hot end to burn through the cord binding his hands. Ingrid was able to move her hands just enough to the side so by looking over her shoulder she could see to get the hot end of the stick onto the cord. It took a while before the smoke rose and the cord started to fray. Baruch was pulling his hands apart as strongly as he could and he was soon able to wriggle his wrists free. He took the stick from Ingrid and shuffled across the floor to throw it back into the fire.

He hurried back to his place with his hands secreted behind his back, just as Voss appeared with an empty bowl. 'You missed out, sonny. That's mighty good grub.' He went through to Pia, who could be heard dishing out more stew. Voss returned without comment and went back down the tunnel to the outside.

Baruch took a small knife out of his boot and cut the knot on his leg bindings. He was careful to keep the rope intact so he could fool his captors if necessary. Kane might appear at any moment. He knew his gun was still under the woodpile where he had kicked it away. Retrieving it, he felt the odds suddenly swinging just a little way in his favour. He freed Ingrid's hands and gave her the gun, indicating to keep it behind her back but not to shoot it unless he said so. It wasn't easy communicating with gags, but

142

it was too dangerous to remove them.

Now he wanted to know where the third tunnel would lead. How far did that go back, and where did it go? He pointed to it and looked at Ingrid. She shook her head; she didn't know anything to help him. Should he go now, or wait? What if Voss came back in, or Kane? Being free of rope was not the end of the game.

He made a quick decision. Weighing up the odds, now that he had his gun, he thought they should make a break for it. But not out of the main tunnel. Not knowing exactly where Voss was positioned outside would give Voss the advantage. He decided they should risk the small stepped tunnel. The smoke suggested it might lead to an air hole and a possible escape route. Very quickly he cut Ingrid free and pulled her towards the opening. He gathered up the rope, grabbed the candle out of the lamp and pulled Ingrid up the couple of steps into the tunnel.

Quickly they followed the twists and turns as far into the rock as they could go. The tunnel was definitely going upwards, hopefully to a shaft. The candle didn't throw out much light and the tunnel began to narrow. Baruch stopped and removed their gags. He said nothing but pressed their lips together. It was the best thing that had happened since he got to the cave. He put a finger on Ingrid's lips so that she didn't speak. He listened carefully in case their escape had already been discovered. But there were no sounds at all.

In his mind at least, if they came after him, he

would snuff the candle and wait until the sounds were near enough, then start shooting. Disastrously, everything changed as they went round the next bend.

The tunnel floor suddenly went downhill, almost vertically. Baruch held the candle over the shaft and peered down. It was no more than twelve or fourteen feet but the candlelight glinted on water. His heart sank. On the other side of the shaft, the tunnel turned into no more than a large fissure in the rock sucking the thin line of smoke towards an inaccessible opening. Baruch tried to hide his disappointment.

'Look,' Ingrid whispered. 'The water is moving; it's not a pit. It looks like a tiny stream and streams have to come out somewhere. Have we got enough rope for me to go down?'

'You?'

'Of course, me. If it doesn't go anywhere you'd be able to pull me up. I'd struggle to get you out of there.'

It was obvious, but Baruch was thinking of protecting Ingrid, not sending her off into the bowels of the earth.

'It's only a few feet,' she said.

Baruch joined the ropes. It was just about long enough; whether it was strong enough would soon be tested. He gave Ingrid the candle, then put the rope round his waist and braced himself. Ingrid eased herself over the edge. She grabbed the rope and slid off into the shaft. For a moment she dangled as the rope swung, Baruch jigged, then stood rock solid. Ingrid steadied herself, put the candle in her mouth and slowly descended hand by hand. The candlelight showed the stream to be no more than a few inches deep; she could see the pebbles. The only way to go was, of course, down-stream.

'I'll go a short distance,' she whispered to Baruch. 'Then I'll come back and tell you.'

Baruch watched the candlelight disappear round a sharp turn to the right. He prayed that Ingrid might see where the stream emerged from the rock. How easy that would be if this was a way out of the cavern and the rockface. He waited. Soon he was in near total darkness. With Ingrid gone his ears began to strain. Could he hear voices, or was it the murmur of the water and the blood in his ears? Light began to flicker in the shaft. Ingrid returned.

'I can't see where it ends, but it doesn't seem to get any deeper. I don't want to come back up.'

It was not an easy decision: once he was down the shaft Baruch realised there would be no getting back out. They were committed to following the stream. Remembering the small watercourse that ran by the willow brakes near the entrance to the cave, Baruch figured this trickle of water must come out some-where not too far away. He would just have to hope the exit hole was not too small.

A moment later he was aware of voices. Somebody would be bound to search this tunnel soon. He should slip away and leave them wondering.

'Go up the steps, Kane, and take a look.'

'I need a lamp for that.'

Baruch didn't wait to hear any more. He dropped the rope and eased himself over the edge, then dropped to the floor. They went downstream quickly, round the corner, with Ingrid sheltering the light to prevent it getting back to the shaft and giving away their position. They stopped and listened. They could hear Kane Benson approaching the shaft.

'Ain't nobody here. They'd be loco to go down the hole. Ain't no way to get out of that.'

This was not good news. It seemed there might be some obstacle or something to prevent their escape. Baruch smiled at Ingrid to reassure her.

'Pay no heed to that. We'll find a way out.' Within himself he was not so sure. 'Let's press on and see where this comes out.'

A couple more twists brought them into a low cavern, and in an instant Baruch saw the problem. The stream ran into a deep water hole and the roof came down to the water level at the furthest end. This was the blockage, a deep pool. The water must eventually get out, but it looked like it just trickled out under the rock. There was no opening big enough for a body to get through. The only way to find out would be to go into the water and hope to find the exit, but the roof was very low and the water looked very black in the candlelight.

Baruch approached the pool slowly and tried to see down into the depths. He could see nothing except the reflection of the light.

'Maybe the other way,' he suggested. 'Let's go back to the shaft and see if there's any way out in the other direction.'

He wasn't hopeful but knew he needed to keep their spirits up.

A few feet away from the shaft they were stopped in their tracks.

Bang! Bang!

Two shots reverberated around the cavern. Then there were voices shouting. More shots. Lots of shooting. A commotion. A scream. More shouting, more shots.

Straining their ears, they could hear people running, scuffling in the dirt, sliding as if taking cover. Things were being thrown. So much shouting. Then shooting in the little tunnel leading to the shaft just ahead of them. The noise was deafening and the acrid smell of black powder was flowing freely across the shaft and out through the fissure with the wood smoke. Baruch told Ingrid to keep the light covered. He drew his gun and crept towards the shaft.

Someone was crawling along the tunnel in the direction of the hole. A moment later he saw the shadowy figure sliding over the edge of the shaft ready to drop to the little stream. Then down he came with a crash. The noise startled Ingrid and the candle illuminated the fallen figure.

Baruch recognised the man lying in the stream immediately.

'Don't move!'

It was Erik, clutching his leg with one hand and holding a pistol with the other. He instinctively raised the gun. Baruch leapt forward and kicked it out of his hand, planting his own gun on Eric's forehead.

'Ingrid, bring the rope. So, you sonofabitch, I should pull the trigger and bring your miserable life to the end it deserves. How could you do this to your own brother and his wife? My ma and pa.'

He swung his boot for a second time, connecting with Erik's ribs. 'That's for the hurt and pain you've caused, Erik Elias. You should be ashamed to carry the same name as decent, hard-working folk. This land will be built on people like us, however many of your kind try to destroy what we build. Your kind are nothing but thieving rattlesnakes, and I'll let a judge and jury show you who wins in the end.'

'Whatever you build, someone will come and take it away,' Erik said, spitting into the water. His face was contorted with the pain in his leg, probably broken in the awkward fall.

Ingrid tied Erik up, while Baruch kept his gun on their prisoner, knowing never to turn his back on a snake.

There was still some noise of people in the cavern, but no more gunshots.

'Hey!' Baruch called out up the shaft, believing it was probably Miller and Mart at least. 'Hey!' He called again. There was no response. He stood in the stream and fired three shots up the shaft.

Footsteps approached. 'Who's down there?'

'It's me, Baruch. I've got Erik, too, and Ingrid.'

Miller appeared at the top of the shaft. 'Well lookee here! Only trouble is there ain't no way out, is there?'

'A rope might help,' Baruch said, hopefully.

'Just joshing,' Miller replied, arms akimbo, a broad smile just caught by the light of the lamp he was holding over the shaft.

A few moments later, a strong rope was dangled into the shaft, and with three men holding it firmly they were brought up one by one: Ingrid first, Erik hogtied next, and finally Baruch.

Back in the cavern they were greeted by a welcome sight. Kane and Voss were roped up and sitting on the ground, both with blood-soaked bandages over gunshot wounds. The woman was also tied but sitting in a chair. Looking quite pleased with themselves, Mart and Sheriff Hempson were just checking their guns and reloading.

Baruch looked at the sheriff for a moment. 'Sheriff Hempson?'

'Yes, son?'

'But I thought . . . They said. . . .'

'Said what? That I was one of them? Who told you that?'

Baruch pointed to Voss. Voss spat in the sand.

'Him,' Hempson said, smiling. 'Of course he would. Eh, Vossy? Mr Snag Hampton, as you were before you changed your name. Thought I was on your side, didn't you? I've had my suspicions about you. Then when Erik, here, came to see you about the Elias shebang, I knew you two were partners. I kept my head down, strung you along good and proper. Me and Marshal Miller.'

Voss spat again.

Hempson turned to Baruch. 'Met up with Bryce Radford at the Siggursons'. Nearly put a hole in each other before we identified ourselves. Radford's out there with Arnie. He's going to bring Abe to Vendigo.' He looked at the forlorn but defiant figures of Erik, Voss and Kane. 'Circuit judge'll be along in a couple weeks. Nice reward going for Erik Elias and Snag Hampton.'

'There's some dollars for the Benson Brothers, too,' Baruch added.

'The spoils of war,' Miller concluded.

But it wasn't quite over yet.

12

Here they all were, sitting in the Vendigo court-house, waiting for the judge to take his seat. Marshal Miller was the chief prosecutor, having been on the tail of Elias and Hampton, now called Voss, for some time.

Sitting in the front row, Baruch was flanked by his ma on the left. His pa was absent, now conscious but still confined to bed. On his other side was Ingrid, with Arnie still sporting some red and bluish bruises on his face, but otherwise on the mend. Behind them were the Gillings, then Bryce Radford and his wife Mary-Lou, who had come to see justice being served. Mary-Lou put her hand on Baruch's shoulder. He turned round and she gave him a broad smile and a nod of the head.

'You see?' she said. 'Faint heart never won fair lady!'

Many residents of Vendigo had turned out to see justice done to the man who had burned out the Elias's supply store and beaten up two of the town's respected citizens. Even Tad had come along with his pal Mart to share in some of the glory. But when all was said and done, the five men standing trial were no more than a handful of misguided and despised ridge riders who found it easier to rob the wealth of others than make an honest and decent living by hard graft.

Erik Elias, Voss – charged under his real name, Snag Hampton – Kane and Abel Benson, and Morgan (deceased) were unanimously found guilty by the twelve upright men of the town for a string of robberies, raids and the Vendigo affair. They were to serve lengthy sentences in the prison in Maple Cross, except for Erik, who would go back to Salt Lake City and the state penitentiary. Erik's woman, Pia, was freed without charge. The business of the day done, the prisoners were taken to Vendigo jail while everyone else retired to the saloons to slake their thirst.

Baruch, his family and friends – including Marshal Miller – were entertained by Sheriff Hempson at the Silver Cactus, where exuberant dancing went on well into the night.

Baruch took Miller aside. He was still puzzling how Miller, Mart and Hempson had got to the cave so quickly when they were at least a day's ride away. Miller told him he'd realised how headstrong Baruch was. He'd set out for Erik's cave as soon as Jake came with the message that Baruch had left the Gillings. Hempson rode to the ranch. Miller had met Mart on the road from Mercer's Hole to

Vendigo and everything followed from that. He couldn't resist giving Baruch a piece of advice:

'You may be smart, son, but don't forget, everyone needs someone to look out for them.'

The next day, Baruch woke early at the Gillings'. He had coffee on the veranda with Jake as the sun rose into a clear blue sky. Reflecting on all the drama of the past few days, his mind was nevertheless drawn to two matters of the future rather than the past. Try as he might, he couldn't stop thinking about Ingrid and Arnie, who were staying at the Silver Cactus. He wanted to be riding into town and taking breakfast with them. But also still asleep at the Gillings', just a few feet away from where he was actually sitting, were his ma and pa. He didn't just see them as his parents, but seeing his ma in court yesterday he realized that their lives had been devastated and he had a responsibility towards securing their future. At the same time he prayed for his pa, prayed that he would pull through and, in good time, be fully fit once more. The sight of two beloved people, seeing them not as his parents but as two elderly folk needing support, was a tough awakening. Somehow he would have to sort out what their future would be.

A little while later, sitting down to breakfast with his ma, he knew he had to raise the subject.

'Ma, when Pa is fully recovered, what are you planning on doing? Where are you going to live?'

Hedda was nibbling on some bacon, the first time she'd eaten meat at breakfast since the fire.

She'd lost a lot of weight and her hair, slightly straggly, seemed to have suddenly turned more like the colour of the silver that miners were hoping was in the nearby hills. Of course it had been turning for years, but Baruch had been away for the last four.

'Eveline and Jethro have said we can stay here as long as we need.'

'That's right kind,' Baruch said smiling across the table at their hosts.

'You're welcome, you know that,' Eveline said to Hedda. 'You take as much time as you need.'

Baruch turned to his ma. 'I guess we can't move Pa until he's proper fit again. Do you want to rebuild?'

Hedda turned to her son, her eyes sparkling with a hard determination like the fire seen in diamonds. 'Of course we do. For more 'an twenty year we've served this community with every darned thing they've ever needed, and some they didn't even know they needed. Flour and salt. Pots, pans and skillets. Wire and posts. Stoves, buckets, sacks and every darned thing. You think we stop just because some firefly burns us out? No, sir.'

She thumped her fist on the table and everyone cheered her defiance. Baruch gave his ma a hug.

'I'm going into town,' he said. 'You take it easy, Ma!'

A plan was forming in Baruch's mind as he rode the couple of miles into Vendigo. His first stop was at the sheriff's office to get something off his mind.

'Sheriff, I owe you an apology. I jumped to con-
clusions about the name Hampton and
Hempson. . . .'

'Forget it, son, it's good to see you. Look here,
now I'm short of a couple of deputies, what would
you say. . . .'

'No,' Baruch replied instantly. 'You're asking the
wrong man. Bring Mart out of retirement.'

'I've already asked him, he's considerin'. Miller
will be going back to Maple Cross where he's based.
He'll escort the prisoners an' I'll be short-handed
again.'

'Thought of asking Jake Gilling?' Baruch suggested. 'Anyway, that's not what I came here for.
There's a bag of reward money for these criminals,
isn't there?'

'Of course,' Hempson replied. 'You'll have a tidy
sum coming your way. And there's the money you
and Bryce took off the Bensons. All that has to be
shared out.'

'I'm thinking of rebuilding my folks' shebang,
bigger an' better, same site, going back further on
the plot.'

'Go and have a word with Mart.'

'Mart?'

'Yes, talk to him.'

Baruch took his leave of Hempson. He called in at
the Silver Cactus to ask after Mart and was directed
to his business premises further along Main Street.
As he read the sign, Hempson's advice became clear.
Mart and Tad. Lumber Yard. As he hitched at the rail,

Tad came out to greet him.

'Heard you done all right, kid.'

Mart followed him out, hand extended. They shook warmly. 'You know my partner Tad, of course.'

'Sure do,' said Baruch, 'an' I've got a job I'd like to talk about.'

On the way back up Main Street he couldn't help himself, stopping at the Silver Cactus. Arnie and Ingrid were saddling up in the yard ready for the ride back to Vimy Point.

'Stay here with your folks as long as you need, Baruch, but I hope you'll be back out with us before too long. We'll have to get them beeves to market soon.'

He helped Ingrid into the saddle. 'Don't you worry, Arnie, wild horses won't keep me here longer than necessary. Just got to sort out with my ma and pa.'

He wished he was riding back with them, but at least Ingrid would be safe with her father riding beside.

Baruch stayed in Vendigo another two days. His pa had regained enough consciousness but, still unable to talk, the doc didn't know if he'd make a full recovery. He didn't tell his ma that he'd instructed Tad and Mart to clear the site and begin rebuilding. He wanted to surprise them in a few weeks' time. With a gang on site, Tad had estimated four to six weeks to clear and rebuild.

So now, everything done, Baruch was free to ride back to Ingrid. He rode two days and a night to

Radford without stopping. He had a great evening with Bryce and Mary-Lou and set out the next day with a song in his heart. Time was marching on. There was a lot of work to be done, hiring casual hands and driving the herd to Maple Cross, then there would be harvesting and hog fattening. Did he want to work the land? It wasn't a decision for him alone.

One evening at dinner, for which Angelina had produced the best stew ever – perhaps she had an inkling of what was on Baruch's mind – Baruch stood up when they'd all finished. He looked at Ingrid and smiled. He smiled at Angelina, and then he looked directly at Arnie.

'Arnie,' he began, 'I've got a question for you.'

'Sit down, son,' Arnie said rather brusquely. 'The question is about a wedding, isn't it?'

Baruch didn't like the way he was being spoken to; it didn't sound like the Arnie he knew. Not wanting to aggravate the mood, he kept quiet and just shrugged.

Arnie slapped the table. 'I've made my decision.'

The atmosphere was suddenly tense. Ingrid turned to her father. She was about to say something but Arnie frowned, and she held back.

'Angelina, will you be my wife?'

A pin falling from the table would have been deafening. A stunned silence greeted this extraordinary request.

Angelina burst into tears. She wanted to say yes, but the word couldn't make its way out past the breathtaking gasps of sheer delight. She put her hand on Arnie's and just nodded instead.

The all broke into peals of laughter. When it subsided, Arnie took Angelina in his arms and gave her a huge hug. Then he turned to Ingrid.

'Ingrid, do you want to marry this headstrong man?'

'Of course I do, Papa.'

One month later, the town of Vendigo Bluff witnessed a very special celebration for the opening of the rebuilt Elias store and a double wedding. Tables lined Main Street, and flags flew from every pole and draping point. Citizens sat down to a great feast thanks to the bounty money and the confiscated dollars that were found in the Bensons' saddle-bags. Baruch's share had provided everything for the celebration, the new store, and enough to enable him to buy up more land around Arnie's ranch if he wanted it.

Before the feast began, Baruch went up to his ma. His pa, now partly recovered, was sitting beside her in a wheelchair, still unable to walk from the beating he'd been given by his brother, and not yet having regained speech.

'There have been two weddings today, Ma, and in my pocket is something from another one. When you were robbed, the Bensons took some jewellery, didn't they?'

His ma looked at him with a tear forming in her eye. She nodded.

'A wedding ring?' Baruch asked.

She held up her hand to show Baruch the thin gold band. The she reached across to her husband and showed that his wedding ring was missing.

Baruch put his hand in his pocket and slipped the ring on his pa's finger. His pa blinked and examined his hand.

Hedda said, 'I don't suppose he even knew it had gone.'

A couple of tears found their way down her cheek as she squeezed her husband's hand. She smiled at Baruch and then turned to her husband, put her arms round his neck and kissed his cheek.

'He'll mend,' she said. 'He'll mend. But we'll need help running the store. Maybe you'd like to come back to Vendigo with your new wife and start up the new business?'

'We'll see, Ma. I've got to help Arnie on the ranch.'

He left it at that. He didn't want to be drawn into making decisions, and anyway he now had a wife to consult!

Vendigo hadn't seen such a day for a long time. The saloons were full to bursting well into the night. Not a shot was fired out of anger all day long. The whole town joined in the happy conclusion to a very upsetting episode.

That night, the Silver Cactus was the venue for two honeymoon couples. Arnie and Angelina were settling down to their first night together, while Baruch and Ingrid were sitting on the edge of the bed with both feeling rather nervous. Ingrid got up and went behind the screen to undress.

'Ma wants me to come back to Vendigo and run the store.'

'What about the ranch?'

Baruch sighed. 'Now's not the time for decisions. I just thought I'd let you know.'

Ingrid changed the subject. 'Did you know what Baruch did in the Bible?'

'I didn't know there was a Baruch in the Bible.'

'Oh, yes, he has a book all of his own.'

'So what did he do? Something useful?'

'Yes, very. After Jerusalem was burnt to the ground, he pledged to help by sending money for the rebuilding and to restore all the treasures. A bit like you've done for your folks. Now, blow out the candle and get into bed.'

She waited until Baruch was in bed and the room lit only by moonlight, then she came out from behind the screen quietly and slipped under the covers.